Embracing My Duty

Copyright

Opening Quote

I am temperamental, and I have imperfections, and I am emotional. I am unpredictable. I am naked. I am vulnerable. I am a woman. I am opening up to you. Love me or leave me. Just take it or leave it. It's not that I'm needy. Just need you to see me. Take me, free me, see through to the core of me. Take me, free me, there will be no more pretending. Now I stand before you with my heart in my hands. I'm asking you to take me just the way that I am. Please lay down your arms. Do you know me, make me feel safe from harm.

I Am by Christina Aguilera

Chapter One

🛡 Krissy 🛡

"Ah!" I scream when Ryland slaps me so hard across the face that I fall backwards. I crash through a table. Air is sucked right out of my body, and for a moment, I feel like my heart ceases to beat.

But freezing is my mistake.

Ryland straddles me and puts his hands around my neck, squeezing. "Think you can just mouth off like that, huh? Embarrass me in front of my friends?" His hands get tighter and tighter until my vision starts to get blurry and dark. I claw at his hands, but it doesn't work. I can't move. I can't breathe. I'm getting weaker and weaker. "You want one of them. Is that it? Is that why you're parading around like a slut?"

"No...," I manage to croak out. My fingers tighten around his wrists, but quickly loosen when his grip gets tighter.

He slaps me twice more while keeping one hand tight around my throat. "Which one is it? Huh? Which one do you want?" Another slap.

I try to shake my head. I suck in air, but it never gets past my throat. Ryland is squeezing too hard. My body feels like it's convulsing. My eyes feel like they're popping out of my sockets. Still, he doesn't let up. I feel his fist against my chest, ribs, and face.

I fade faster and faster until I can't feel anything anymore. He gets darker and darker. His voice gets further and further away until I'm floating. Higher and higher into a pitch black and lonely world...

◠◡◠

"Ah!" I shriek when I wake up. My hands immediately fly to my throat as I gasp in breath after breath, but I can't get enough air.

I frantically look around the room as I feel my body for scratches and injuries. Nothing looks familiar. Where am I? I'm not in my room. I'm not in Ryland's. The walls are white. There's nothing in the room but a dresser and nightstand.

I throw the covers off and feel my legs for any injuries. My heart is racing so fast, I can hear it like a Nascar race going on in my head. More screams are trying to escape, but they won't come with the massive amounts of air I'm sucking down.

Several moments later, things start coming into focus. Air begins to fill my lungs and circulate through me. I don't feel like I'm choking anymore, and the race car engines begin to go away. Eventually, all that's left is my own ragged breathing. I hug myself as tears I didn't know I was crying fall down my cheeks. I don't bother wiping them.

I curl my knees to my chest and wrap my arms around my legs. I lean my head on my knees. I have to reorient myself.

"I'm not in the psych ward...," I whisper to myself. "I'll never be there again." I shake my head. "Ryland isn't here. I'm safe." I look around my bedroom. "Beige walls. Warm and inviting. Not white. I have a closet and dresser. I have two nightstands." I nod as I talk myself through. "My carpet is fluffy, soft, and beige to match the walls. My bed is a Queen. It's nice and soft. My sheets are soft and a warm beige color. My blanket is dark brown." The more I talk, the more I calm down. "There's art on the walls. So different from the psych ward. So different from my old place or Ryland's." I let out a long breath as I start to regain control of myself. "I'm okay. I'm safe. He doesn't know where I am. He's in jail. He can't get me here."

But he can. I know he can. He hasn't been released yet, but he could easily find out where I am. He still has powerful contacts.

I shake my head to rid the thoughts. "No. I changed my entire identity. I'm not the same person anymore."

I look at the clock on my nightstand. It's only 2:30am, but I know damn well I'm not going back to sleep. Not after a nightmare like that. Instead, I get up and let my toes curl into the soft carpet underneath me. After a few moments, I stand and head for the shower.

I love my house. My grandparents gave it to me last year.

Almost an entire year after I left Ryland.

The house is untraceable to me or my grandparents. I wouldn't be alive without them. They're the only ones I'm still in contact with. I lost all my friends and family when I grew a backbone and went to my grandparents for help.

I put a fist to my chest as I step into the hot shower. I'm not thinking about it. I won't. I have a new life now. The life I deserve. I'm on my own in a beautiful house near a small lake that I can see from almost every window in the house. It feels like I'm in the mountains, not on the outskirts of small-town Piper Falls, Texas. There are enough trees around me to make me feel secluded and protected from every aspect of life outside my walls.

I keep to myself. I don't talk to anyone and rarely go into town for anything. I use a delivery service for my groceries and everything else.

Truth is, it's not easy to leave my house. This is my safety. My therapist, who I see online, says it's agoraphobia. I didn't know what that really was until he explained it. It doesn't all have to do with being around people and having anxiety and panic in crowds. Sometimes, the idea of leaving the house for people is anxiety and panic inducing enough.

That's where I am. I can't go outside at all most days. I watch the world go by from behind glass. I watch my large German Shepherd dog run around the yard from my window. I tried standing in my doorway, but I can't even do that.

Despite that, I'm working on it. My therapist, a nice older man named Jim, gives me goals. Sometimes, I'm able to reach them. Sometimes, I'm not. It's when I'm not that I get really down on myself. How hard is it to just go outside and stick to my yard? Why can't I walk ten steps from my door?

Jim says it's because nothing bad happened to me inside this house. All of the attacks happened at Ryland's and my old house. I associate anything outside my four walls as dangerous. Opening my door here, the one I feel safe behind, is opening me up to something not safe.

I wrap a towel around myself after I get out of the shower and shut off the water. I'm drying off when I hear whining. My heart sinks. I hurry out of my ensuite bathroom and quickly open my bedroom door.

I kneel down and let my German Shepherd, Killer, see me as I wrap my arms around him. "I'm so sorry you couldn't get in. I don't know why I closed my door all the way. I must've been out of it last night. I'm sorry, baby boy." I never do that. Most of the time, Killer is in my bed with me.

He nuzzles me and instantly calms and centers me. Had I left the door open a crack for him like I usually do, I probably would've been far more calm a lot faster than I was able to make myself when I woke up.

"I'm sorry, Killer. You were probably so worried."

I stand and walk to my dresser to get some clothes for the day. After I get dressed in shorts and a tank top, I walk back to my bathroom to brush out my hair. Killer watches me closely, but he doesn't move from where he's decided to sit. It's in the center of my room where he can see everything, including what I'm doing in the bathroom.

I chuckle as I come back out. "So protective, aren't you?"

His brown eyes seem to glimmer as he tilts his head. I scratch behind his ears and head for the door, but he hurries to block me.

I furrow my brows. "What are you doing? Don't you want breakfast?"

He narrows his eyes at me and nudges my leg hard enough to make me step back.

"Killer! Enough. Come on. Let's go downstairs." I try to step around him, but he's not having any of it. "What has gotten into you?

Killer nudges me back again. Confused, I let him just because I'm curious about what he's trying to say.

Once the backs of my legs hit the bed, I glance over my shoulder. Killer sits, and I laugh. "You want me to go back to bed?"

His ears perk, and he pants a moment before tilting his head.

"Fine. But you're cuddling with me."

If I didn't know better, I'd swear he understands every word I say. He jumps on the bed and waits for me. I shake my head with a smile and crawl back into bed. I burrow under the covers and yawn as Killer lies down next to me. I turn on my side and wrap my arms around the large animal with soft fur and crazy instincts.

"I don't know what I'd do without you," I whisper.

He smacks his lips a few times before settling himself with his head resting on top of mine. I bury my face into his neck and chest. Like magic, I fall into a peaceful sleep. One I only seem to attain if he's here. It's like I trust that he'll keep me safe, so I'm able to relax around him. Even if I do have a nightmare, he calms me quickly, and I trust that.

Maybe he's the secret. Maybe if he's near, I can venture out a further distance from my house than just the front doorframe.

I take a deep breath and inhale his clean dog scent. Before I know it, I find myself fading into a blissfully dreamless sleep.

♡ ♡ ♡

When I wake up again, Killer is nudging me and whining, but he's still lying in the same position we fell asleep in. I glance at my clock with a yawn. It's 9:30am. I'm sure the poor thing has to relieve himself.

"Wow, I slept so long." I sit up. Killer, panting happily, leaps off the bed after me when I get up. "I'm sure you need to go potty, huh?"

As soon as we're out of my bedroom, he takes the lead and prances down the stairs. I laugh and let him out the back door, glancing towards the woods to the right of my house as I bite my lip. While he's out, I prepare his food. I always get him Fresh Pet food. He likes it a lot and enjoys seeing me take it out of the fridge. I'm happy to spend the money to get it for him. Especially since it keeps him healthy.

Once I have the food in his bowl, I start preparing my own breakfast. I love oatmeal in the morning. Butter and brown sugar is my favorite, but sometimes, like today, I really want a banana. After I mix some water into my oatmeal and add the butter and brown sugar, I cut the banana up. Killer hasn't barked to be let in yet, so I let him be and start eating as I scroll through the news on my phone.

After twenty minutes, I am finishing my oatmeal and furrow my brows at Killer still not barking to be let in. I put my bowl in the sink and head to the door.

"Killer!" I call after opening it. I snap my head to my right when I hear him bark. "Come on inside!" Another bark, closer this time, before a brown fur missile comes bolting around the corner of the house. "Where have you been?"

Killer barks and nuzzles into me. I pat his head and run my fingers through his fur as he runs inside. I laugh and start stepping back into the house as I close the screen but stop dead in my tracks, frozen.

"He came to visit again" a tall man wearing worn jeans that fit him just right and a dark blue t-shirt that shows off every single muscle he has says to me as he saunters around the corner of my house and walks towards me.

"U-um… s-sorry…" I step back as my heart quickens. I know who he is. It's Caden Andrews. He's a cop with Piper Falls Police Department.

A cop.

Like him and his friends.

"He found me in my yard," he drawls with a huge grin. His voice is deep with a thick Southern accent.

"Th-thank you." I quickly step back and close the screen before slamming the heavy, wooden door closed and slapping the bolt lock in place. I lock the handle and immediately start thinking of how many more locks I should buy to make myself feel safe. I rub my chest as I lean against the door.

He's a cop. A fucking cop. Cops aren't safe. They're power hungry assholes who only look out for their friends, especially those who hold that Thin Blue Line with them.

So, why don't I feel immediate fear when I see him? Why does my heart skip several beats when he's near? Why do I always look towards his house when I let Killer outside or when I'm in my office that looks towards his property?

Why do I feel safer knowing he's near?

And why, oh why, is he the object of all of my fantasies?

Chapter Two

♡ Caden ♡

I watch the girl jump back into her house and sigh.

Krissy Wright.

I know nothing about her other than she's my neighbor, she has a large German Shepherd who seems to have taken a liking to me, and she's beautiful. Other than that, all I know is she's fucking skittish, private as hell, and seemingly hates human contact. No one in town that I've talked to knows much about her either, which makes me more and more curious.

Especially since I'm a cop. I should be able to find information about this girl.

Not that I have any reason for it other than I'm a cop. I'm naturally curious about people, but when someone is so mysterious, it usually means they have something to hide. It's that single thing that bothers the hell out of me. I don't like not knowing things. It makes the cop in me go fucking crazy.

I scrub a hand down my face and turn around. I head back to my house, but it's truly a struggle because I have so many questions about this girl. I have a very real feeling that she's on the run. Call it cop instincts, but something is off.

I don't live that far away from the mysterious woman. If she has lights on at night, I can see them through the trees, but we live far enough away that we both still have as much privacy as we want.

I'm lost in her mystery when I get back to my house and am surprised to see Mateo Fernando, my best friend, waiting for me. Mateo is a Sergeant with the investigations unit of Piper Falls Police Department. We've been friends since we were kids and went through the police academy together. We have a few other friends that we grew up with who also went through the academy with us, but Mateo and I have a much deeper bond, though neither of us really know why.

"Did you forget the day? Why aren't you ready to go, Lieutenant?" Mateo asks with a teasing smirk. I'm a Lieutenant with the Patrol Division. Like him, I work Monday through Friday from nine in the morning to five in the evening. We're on call on the weekends and often go into work on the weekdays together.

I give him a cocky grin. "You know me. Had to get some ass before I start my day."

"Yeah, I don't buy it. You'd be in town if you were hooking up. Not sneaking through the woods. Hurry up. I want my fucking coffee."

I roll my eyes, but jog into the house. I'd started to get dressed, but when I heard Krissy's dog bark, I went outside to say hi. I decided to bring him back to his house and throw a stick or two on the way because he gave me an excuse to see the beautiful woman whose beautiful green eyes haunt my damn dreams.

When I finish getting dressed in my trademark jeans and dark dress shirt, I head out of my bedroom, grabbing my gunbelt. I put it on on my way downstairs and head outside. I jump in his vehicle after locking my door, and he takes off out of my driveway.

On the way by Krissy's house, I can't help but keep my eyes on the trees that keep her house from view from the road. Leave it to Mateo to immediately pick up on it.

"Is that where you came from?"

I sigh and rub my head. "Yeah. I was returning her dog."

"No change?"

"No. She pretty much leaped in her house the second she saw me."

Mateo sighs. "She's definitely a mystery. No one knows anything about her, other than the fact that she moved here a year ago and barely leaves her house for anything."

I look over at him. "Have you found anything else out about her at all? There's just something about her." I glance out the window again. "Something doesn't sit right with me. The way she looks at me fucks me up."

"Like she's afraid of you."

"Yep, but it's more than that. It's like she's hiding something and is afraid to let her guard down, but I really don't think it's anything illegal. I just think she's running from something really bad."

"I know we talked about this before, and you don't agree, but have you thought anymore about the theory that she's on the run from law enforcement and is afraid you'll find out if you keep snooping around?"

I shake my head, immediately dismissing the idea. "She knows I'm a cop. I don't think she'd stick around if she was on the run from cops. And that also insinuates that she did something illegal, which I just really don't believe she did. Nothing about her gives me that feeling at all. I think she's scared of something or someone, but she won't let me get close enough to really talk to her about anything."

"I can keep digging, but I don't have anything to go on."

"I know, man. I've been trying, too."

We both fall silent on the rest of the drive into town. Mateo stops at Cozy Bean Cafe, and we both get out of his Bronco. We head inside in silence. It's pretty busy, but that's normal for this time of morning. Maybe people are getting their morning coffee and pastries before going to work. I'm here every day, sometimes more than once.

We wait in line as others place their orders. When it's our turn, we order our coffees and move to the side to wait. I take a bit of my cream filled donut and hold back the moan threatening to escape.

"Fuck, that's good," I rumble appreciatively.

"It wouldn't be a morning if I didn't hear you say that." Mateo grins as he eats his apple fritter.

"I think I need to get one of those later."

Mateo laughs. "Playing right into those stereotypes, aren't we?"

I laugh. "Hey. I'll do it if they taste like this."

"Hey, before I take off. Does anyone here know a woman that goes by the name of Phoenix Rivers?" a deep male voice with an accent absolutely not from around here asks Jake, the barista who basically lives in this cafe. "She's about five feet. Tiny girl. Blonde hair. Pretty green eyes."

Jake grins. "Dude, you just described half the women population of this town." He points to a woman sitting near a window scrolling through her phone. "Like her."

The guy laughs after glancing over his shoulder. He's got a babyface. He's clean-shaven and clean cut. He's wearing black slacks, dress shoes, and a white shirt with a red and black striped tie. His hair is dark blond, eyes are blue.

"Fair point." He hands Jake a card. "If you happen to see her, give me a call."

Jake glances at the card and nods with a charming grin and wink. "Sure thing, officer."

Mateo and I watch in silence as the officer walks out of the coffee shop taking a sip of his drink. "Tell me that didn't seem weird as fuck," I say.

"I'd be lying. That guy's not from around here. Midwest accent."

"Minnesota," I say confidently, finally placing it. "Remember that domestic violence training we went to in Minneapolis?"

"You're right."

"Here you go, guys," Jake says, putting mine and Mateo's coffee up on the counter.

We both walk to the counter and take our cups. "Who was that guy?" I ask Jake.

"A cop from Minneapolis PD. Don't know what the hell he's doin' way down here." He hands me the card the cop gave to him. He lowers his voice. "Never heard of no one named Phoenix, but that description was fucking generic."

"Mind if we keep this?" Mateo asks.

"All yours." Jake puts a couple more drinks on the counter and calls out a couple names.

"Jake, do you know anything about Krissy Wright?" I ask on a whim. I have a really bad feeling, but I'm not willing to say anything about it right now.

"Uh. That girl out by you?" He finishes making another drink and puts it on the counter. "Not a lot. I know she orders a lot. Food and groceries. I've taken her some of our baked goods and coffee a few times."

I nod. "What do you make of her? Has she told you anything about herself?"

He pauses as he sets another drink that someone hands him on the counter. "Now that I think about it, I did have a strange encounter with her a few days ago. She grabbed her order. It was just a latte and some plain bagels with cream cheese, but she seemed a little out of it. Like she hadn't slept. I asked if she was okay, and her response was to ask me if I ever felt like I was stuck in one event in time and couldn't get out of it. I didn't know how to really respond, but she cut me off anyway. She smiled and shook her head. She apologized and just said she's tired and didn't sleep well. Then thanked me for bringing her stuff to her."

"Has she said anything at all any other times?" Mateo asks.

"She doesn't say a lot, but I did ask her how she was the last time she placed an order. She said she was doing okay and working on getting out a little more each day. I asked her if she had some issues getting herself to go places. She told me she had some agoraphobia and PTSD from an incident that happened back home, but she didn't say where that was."

"What about her accent?" I ask him. "Anything familiar about it?"

He shakes his head. "No. It's fucking unique, though. It sounds like that guy's did, but there's a Southern undertone, so it throws me. I asked where she was from once, and she told me it doesn't matter. She won't ever go back. Other than those things, though, she's not forthcoming. She usually just says hi to me, thanks me, and we both go about our day."

"Thanks, man. Looks like they're getting slammed." I nod behind him.

He grins. "Yeah. This place would fall apart without me."

Mateo and I laugh as we turn to head out. We get back in his Bronco and head to Headquarters. "I can't even begin to tell you how bad of a feeling I got, but it's almost counteracted by the fact that I think I just had a bunch of pieces put in place for me."

"You think she's this Phoenix Rivers girl?"

I nod. "Yep. He's right. Krissy's accent is unique, but I wouldn't say it's a Southern undertone. I say it's more a Southern accent with a Northern undertone."

"Like… Somewhere and Minnesota…" Mateo whistles through his teeth. "That makes a lot of fucking sense." He pulls into our gated parking lot reserved for police and fire department officials only and parks in a spot reserved for me. We both share it if we carpool like this. If we don't, then he parks in a regular place, but my spot is closer to the front, and we don't have to walk far to get to the building.

"I'm gonna look some shit up. I can't shake this damn feeling."

"Well, you know I trust your instincts. I have a case I'm working on, but if you need me, just holler."

"For sure."

We enter through the garage and walk to the door leading to a hallway that connects right to the bullpen. The second we enter, my feeling gets even worse. My chest tightens, and I don't have a damn clue why.

The second I'm seated behind my desk and hear a knock on my door, though, I understand. The front desk receptionist is standing in the doorframe of the door I haven't closed. I usually don't unless I want to be left alone.

"Hey, Lieutenant," she says. She's a sweet older woman who always spoils us with lunch and baked goods. "I know you just got in, but this officer is from Minnesota. He'd like to speak with you."

I meet the cold eyes of the same cop I saw at Cozy Bean. I narrow mine specifically to show who the Alpha in this situation is. "How can I help you, officer?" I don't get up. Instead, I flick my eyes to a chair. I already don't like him. There's something off about his entire being.

"Good morning, sir. Your receptionist said you're the man I need to talk to." He holds out his hand for me to shake, but I just look at it. Southern hospitality isn't a thing when I know something here is fucked up.

"Sit." I say.

His eyes darken, and I know immediately he hates being told what to do, but he does what I say anyway as he clears his throat. "I'm looking for a woman. Phoenix Rivers. I've been able to track her somewhere around here or the Waco or Austin area. Honestly, I'm pretty sure she's in

15

Wako, but I'm covering all my bases here." He gives me a smile I'm sure he thinks is charming, but I've been doing this a long time.

"You got a picture? The name doesn't sound familiar, and I know everyone in this town."

"Looks like the receptionist did pick the right man. Phoenix would've moved here probably within the past couple of years."

Like a punch to my stomach, I instinctively know who he's talking about, but I don't lead on that I know anything. Nothing but a dumb cop. I lean forward and shake my head. "If she moved here a couple years ago, I'd definitely know. I make it a point to know everyone. If a new girl moved in, the town would be buzzing with that information. We had a new college student move to town a couple weeks ago, and it was like the greatest thing that happened to this town. Everyone was bringing him welcome gifts and certificates to come try their place. Actually, the Cozy Bean gave him a month of free coffee."

"Damn. Yeah, I don't think she'd come here. I've asked a few people already this morning. She'd be quiet as hell. Probably wouldn't draw attention to herself."

I grin. "That in itself would draw suspicion from me. People who go out of their way to try and keep to themselves are hiding something. I don't like things being hidden in my town."

He laughs. "I'm with ya there."

"I didn't catch your name. You got a card or something? If I hear anything, I can let you know. What's up with this chick anyway? Anything I need to know?"

"Actually, yeah." He hands me a card from his wallet. Ryland Evans. An officer with the Minneapolis Police Department. Same one from the Cozy Bean. I knew that, but verification is always nice. "She took a huge chunk of money from an elderly couple up in Elk River. I caught the case because that elderly couple is my grandparents. The trail went cold up there, so I've been doing my own digging. She's definitely a little fraudster. Innocent looking, but some of her wires are twisted. She's cold and very calculating."

"That's fucked up. Damn. And you tracked her down here?"

"Yeah, I found some of her contacts in the Waco area. Old college friends she keeps in contact with. They attended the same sorority and kept close. She has an uncle in Austin, but they haven't really talked in a while.

At least according to him. Piper Falls isn't too far away from either of those places, so I was thinking it might be a good place for her to lie low."

I nod as if I'm in total agreement with him. "Makes sense. Well, I'll tell you what. I'll keep in touch. No promises. I really don't think she's here. No way to hide in a small town, but I'll definitely let you know if anything comes up, or if she turns up."

"I'd appreciate it, man. All I care about is getting my grandparents their money back."

"Happy to bring down a criminal. You got a pic?"

"Oh, shit. Yeah." He pulls out his wallet again and hands me a picture. I don't look at it right away because gut instinct is telling me I already know.

I stand and reach out a hand. "Nice meeting you, Officer Evans. I'll be in touch."

He grasps my hand a little too tightly, like he has something to prove. "Thanks, Lieutenant Andrews. I appreciate the help."

I grin and drop his hand. "Happy to help a fellow brother in blue. Let me show you out." I gesture for him to leave my office, then lead him to the door. I let him back out to the lobby. "Have a great day now, ya hear?" I lay on my thickest and most charming accent. It doesn't just work on women. It works on men, too.

As I expected him to, Ryland grins back and nods. I can tell he doesn't suspect a damn thing. I want to watch him leave, but I don't want him to think I give a shit, so as soon as he's through the door and in the lobby, I close the door behind him and walk to my office.

"Mateo!" I bark. He looks up, sees my demeanor, and jumps up from his desk.

"What happened? Why the fuck was that cop here?" Mateo sits down in the chair Ryland just vacated.

I glance at the photo, and my heart sinks as I turn it towards him so he can see. "Meet Phoenix Rivers."

Our eyes fall on the gorgeous blond with green eyes. Petite. Definitely barely over five feet. Part of me can't believe my luck. I've been trying to figure things out about Krissy since she first moved here.

The other part of me knows the mystery I've been trying to unravel just got harder and a lot more intricate.

"Looks like the girl he was describing at Cozy."

"It's Krissy Wright."

He stares at me in disbelief for a few moments before leaning back and locking his fingers behind his head. "No."

"Yep." I mimic his position as I lean back, and we stare at each other. "Krissy Wright is Phoenix Rivers."

Chapter Three

♡ Krissy ♡

I jump nearly a mile in the air when I hear a knock on my door. My eyes snap to it. Killer starts barking. I grip my chest as my heart starts immediately beating faster. I didn't order anything. No one has any reason to be here, and I don't know anyone. I like it that way. It's for the best.

Another knock has me careening off the edge of oblivion, and I drop from the couch. I lay on the floor with a blanket over my head as Killer growls next to me.

Another knock, harder this time, and I'm hyperventilating. "Krissy?" a deep, commanding voice says. "Krissy, come on! Open up!"

Killer barks and snaps at the door as I curl up tighter. Flashes of my old life roll like the Texas thunder through my mind. Ryland standing over me screaming. The kicks, hits, punches, and sinister glares flow through my head like the tumultuous Rio Grande.

I swallow the screams threatening to escape. I stay as silent as possible, gripping the blankets tightly as I tremble. Killer continues to growl protectively, but he makes no move to leave me.

"Krissy? It's Caden Andrews! Your neighbor! Listen, I know you're probably scared, but you need to answer the door! It's important!"

Caden? Why is Caden here?

I don't move an inch. It's a trick. He's trying to get me to answer the door so he can hurt me. I know better. Never trust a cop. Never. They all protect each other.

Caden is different, the little voice in my head assures me.

I won't listen. She doesn't know what she's saying. She must've forgotten all we've been through. Ryland's friends coming after me after I got a restraining order against him.

Caden's different.

I shake my head and cover my ears. Ryland started out different, too. He treated me like a queen, his queen. It's a trick. It's all a trick.

"Okay, Krissy. You don't need to answer. I won't push it, but I'm not leaving. I'll be out here in my truck watching out for you."

"Oh my God," I whisper.

But I still don't make a motion to leave. I breathe through my panic and squeeze my eyes shut, but it's a huge mistake because all I see is Ryland.

"That's what you want, huh?" he growls as he holds me down.

I fight against him, but I'm weak. Blurs of movement catch my eye, but I can't focus on any one thing. There's pain. There's the fact that I can't move. I'm weak. I can't see clearly. Even Ryland's voice sounds slowed down, even though everything around me is going fast. People are laughing, but the laughs sound demonic.

"Stop...," I plead to everyone and no one at once. "Please..." I feel tears streaming down my face.

Nothing stops.

The pain gets worse.

The laughing mocks me.

My face stings. My lips are puffy, and it feels like I've been stung by multiple bees all at the same time all over my body. I'm fading faster and faster until, blessedly, everything finally goes dark.

I don't know how long I lay on the floor locked in my own mind, but I'm woken up by Killer licking me and softly whining. I blink a few times and see it's already after 10pm. Which means I've been out for almost four hours.

"I'm so sorry, Killer. You're probably dying to get outside."

He licks me and prances towards the front door.

"Killer, come on. Let's go out the back."

He sits by the front door and whines as he looks at me. I haven't forgotten that Caden said he was going to be outside in his truck. Why?

I sigh and walk to the front door. I pull the curtains back just enough so I can look outside. Sure enough, there's a truck in my driveway that I'd recognize anywhere. A Navy blue Ford F150 that I'm sure is brand new. If it's not, there's no way it's more than a couple of years old.

It's a truck I've pictured on more than one occasion parked in my driveway while the owner exits and sweeps me off my feet. He rocks my world night after night and keeps the nightmares at bay. He protects me every second of the day while treating me like I should be. With respect and love. Longing and desire.

I lean my head against the door and take a deep breath. "This isn't easy, Killer." I look down at him. "I'm relying on your instincts here."

He nuzzles my hand like he's telling me to trust him. Killer is the only being in this world, other than my grandparents, that I do trust.

I take another breath and unlock the door slowly. I open it just enough to let him out, then slam it closed and lock it once more.

He's a cop. He's a cop.

The words run in circles through my brain trying to drown out the other voice saying Caden is different.

I peek out the window and see Caden playing with Killer. I smile softly and fight the urge to open the door to see what he wants, but I shake my head at myself. If I've learned one thing over the course of my life, it's to never trust anyone except my grandparents. They've never let me down and have always been around for me when no one else was.

A few minutes later, Killer barks at the door. I peek out the window once more and see Caden getting back in his truck. When he closes the door, I open my door enough for Killer to get in. I still don't know why he's here, but I'm starting to believe more and more that he's not here to hurt me.

"Come on, Killer," I say as I lock the door. Killer follows me as I lock my windows.

Not that glass would stop him if he wanted to get in here. It might be hard to break the glass. When I moved in, I asked for my windows to be redone. My grandparents own this house, but when they gave it to me, they made it look like it was sold to a real estate company. The real estate company, after hearing of the situation, agreed to help and keep the property in their files as them owning it.

I don't pretend to understand. All I know is that Ryland knows nothing about this place, and if he does eventually find out about it, it'll take him a very long time to ever figure out I live here. My grandparents made it look like they have nothing to do with this place.

At least that's what they've told me, and I have no reason not to trust them. If it weren't for them, I'd be dead. I'm sure of it.

Once I'm sure everything is locked, I glance out the window in my extra bedroom. It faces the driveway. I expected Caden to leave, but he's still there. I'm both uneasy and relieved. I can explain the uneasy feeling. That's easy. I can't explain the relieved part of it. I don't know why I feel like I can trust him.

The last thing I'll ever do is trust myself again, though. I trusted Ryland. I was completely blinded by him. I thought he was a good guy. Every time he hurt me, I believed him when he said he was sorry and wouldn't ever do it again. I believed he'd change. I believed in all the moves he made. It all made me believe that time would be different. It never was.

Trusting is for fools. I won't ever be a fool again.

I curl up in bed after I change into a pair of short shorts and a tank top. I pull the blankets up. Knowing I need him, Killer jumps onto the bed and snuggles down as I take out my tablet. I pull up my reading app and select a book in my library to read, *Drunk With Love* by Jason Handler.

He's my favorite author, and I've been looking forward to this release for months. It's a best friends to lovers, and I love that trope. As soon as he announced it was coming, I shamelessly jumped on the preorder. It released at midnight on the East Coast. I'm lucky I don't have to wait until midnight.

I get comfortable and start reading. As usual, I get so wrapped up in the book, that everything else around me fades into nothing. It's just me and the world he created. It's so peaceful and comforting to get so lost in the words on the page.

♡♡♡

I'm surprised once more when I wake up to sun pouring through my bedroom window and Killer licking my face.

I groan and try to bat him away. I don't know when I fell asleep, but I hate feeling like all I do is waste my day. I used to go out a lot to walk. I'd get a coffee. I used to have a good job as a physical therapist that I loved. I used to like doing things outside. Now, I'm a prisoner behind my own walls and in my mind.

Killer doesn't relent, so I yawn and get up. "Fine. You win. Jerk."

Killer jumps down from the bed panting happily. I open the door, and he bounds out of the bedroom and down the stairs. Again, he goes to the front door. I sigh and peek out the curtained window by the door. Caden's truck is still out there, and my heart skips a beat. I nibble my lip more confused than ever. I let Killer out. I can't figure out if I should fear this man, or if I should ask what's going on. Is he stalking me, or protecting me from something?

"Dammit," I growl under my breath as I close and lock the door. I decide to call my grandmother, my voice of reason, and talk to her. I pick up my phone and dial her number on my way to the kitchen.

"Hello, sweet angel. Good morning," my grandmother answers, her voice filled with sugary kindness. She's a typical old woman. She's in her eighties, but still fairly active and independent. Grandpa is still pretty tall, only slightly hunched. They both have graying hair but are the most adorable humans I know.

I let out a sigh, instantly feeling calmer. "Hi, Gram. I've missed your voice."

"Awe, sweetheart. I've missed you, too." She's half Norwegian and half Swedish with a Northern Minnesota accent that I miss so much. "How's the South treating you?"

"It's been warm. Ungodly. We've been reaching crazy temps this entire summer so far. Like if you walk outside, you're instantly drenched in sweat and praying for death."

Grandma laughs. "It's been pretty humid here. The mosquitoes are terrible."

I giggle. "I'd hate for you to see them here. They're bigger and travel in a group. And I mean a group of thousands. You can hear them buzzing at night. It's so gross. You basically have to douse yourself in bug spray. *All* of the bug repellent at one time. All of them. I'm pretty sure they could pick up a whole human and carry them away to their mosquito den."

"Oh my goodness! You've never told me about them before!"

"It's best to not be outside if they can be heard."

"Ick. I don't remember them being that bad when Grandpa and I went down there."

"I think this is the worst year for them. I don't remember them like this either." I pause and reach for Killer's food. I start putting it in a dish when my heart starts racing a little again. I take a deep breath to calm myself before I finally speak again. "Gram, I actually called because I need some advice."

"Of course, sweetheart. What do you need?"

"Well, I've told you about the police officer who lives near me. I've had very little contact with him and kept my distance from people. I mostly get deliveries. I've only been to the town once and really didn't stick around. I just needed to check if places deliver. Anyway… um… Caden and I haven't had much contact. I've only seen him a handful of times. I've beelined back into the house when he's brought Killer back."

"Okay…"

"Well, yesterday morning, he brought Killer back. I thanked him before jumping back into the house, but after dinner last night, he knocked on my door. I freaked out because I wasn't expecting an order or anything. I didn't answer the door even after he announced himself. He said something was important. I still didn't answer. He said I didn't have to. He'd be outside in his truck. I passed out from panic, and when I came to, it was after ten. Killer needed to go outside. Caden was still out there, but he made no attempt to come to the house or try to get in. He just played with Killer for a little while. I just let him out now and Caden was still there. I don't know what to do."

Grandma is silent for long enough that I question if she hung up on me. When I finally hear her breath, I let out a relieved one of my own. "Sweetheart, I was going to call you anyway. Actually, I had my phone in my hand when you called. It startled me. Let me put this on speaker so you can talk to Grandpa, too."

I'm instantly on alert and stand tall. "Gram? What's happening? Pahpa?"

"Hey there, sunshine. There's no easy way to put this," my grandfather's kind and gentle voice comes over the line.

"Pahpa? What's happening?"

"Listen, honey. Ryland is out of jail. They released him yesterday. We just heard it on the news."

My eyes widen. I nearly drop Killer's dish on the floor but manage to get it to the counter. "Oh my God, what? He's not supposed to be released for two more years!"

"I know. They said good behavior as the reason. He's still on probation for five years and is ineligible for hire with police departments."

"He has friends. He could find out where I am!" My eyes snap to the door. "Is that why Caden is here? Is Ryland here?"

"I don't know, sweetheart, but I think we need to hire you some private security. I know of an excellent firm called Prestige Guardians."

"Whatever you think, Pahpa. I've basically shutdown right now. Short circuited. Caden is out there. Is he with Ryland? Did Ryland come here?"

Grandma clears her throat. "I'm just going on instinct here, sunshine, but something about him screams that he's trying to help. If he were working with Ryland, I have no doubt he'd have tried to break in or that Ryland would be with him. And Killer is a very good judge of character. Very protective. I know you have trust issues, but I think you need to trust him. I have a good feeling about him."

I nod before realizing they can't see me. "Yes, ma'am."

"Now, you talk to that man and see what's going on. Trust your dog if you can't trust yourself. Killer has always been very protective of you. I've been comforted knowing he's been with you down there."

"Yes, ma'am." I do trust her. She never liked Ryland. She never met him, just heard about him, but she still didn't like him. I got Killer the year before I moved here. He was one then and had to stay with my grandparents until my landlord approved him being with me. That never happened. Ryland interfered. I ended up with my grandparents after the institution. Killer is three now, and the protective nature has only grown stronger.

"I'll call you as soon as I have security lined up," Grandpa says.

"Yes, sir."

We say our goodbyes and love yous before hanging up. My mind is firmly on Ryland. I should've known he'd find me. Nothing stays perfect forever...

Chapter Four

♡ Caden ♡

I hear Krissy's door open and can't help when I glance up. She's so beautiful, it takes my breath away. She's wearing short sleep shorts and a thin button up shirt over what I can see is a tank top. She wraps the shirt around herself with one arm and pauses by the door.

Killer gives up on me and prances toward his mom. I don't blame him. If I woke up next to the gorgeous woman he gets to every single morning, I don't think I'd ever leave the house.

Sensing her nervousness, I give her my most friendly smile with a nod as I get back into my truck. I didn't really count on staying in my truck all night long. I planned on talking to her about Ryland Evans to see if she knew him. I already know the answer, and that's the reason I didn't intend on leaving her house. I felt an overwhelming urge to stick around to keep her safe, and that instinct hasn't faded.

I'm sore, tired, and fucking starving, but I crawl back into my truck anyway. I don't want her to be scared. After everything I read on Phoenix Rivers, though, Krissy has every reason to be afraid of people, especially the police.

So, I close my door and wait for her to make her move. She closes her door, visibly taking a giant, deep breath. Killer bounces around her as she turns around. With her eyes focused on the cup she's now holding with both hands, Killer leads the way to my truck as happy as a dog can be.

He jumps up on my truck. I have the window down because it's already hot as hell, and the sun has barely risen. July in Texas sees undeniable heat, but this year has been hotter than usual. I scratch behind his ears as he pants happily and wags his tail furiously. I keep my eyes on Krissy. She stops near my truck. Close enough to reach me if she wanted to, but far enough away that she can run if she needs to.

"Hi…," she says barely above a whisper.

I grin. "Hey. How did you sleep?"

She blinks a few times. "Um… actually, I slept really well…" she clears her throat. "I'll revisit that later. Um… I brought you some coffee…" She holds it out to me as Killer jumps back down and trots off. She watches him in awe while I grab the cup.

"Thank you," I say. I can't help but notice it's in one of those reusable to go cups that's insulated and has a lid. I take a drink and groan appreciatively as the bitter liquid slides down my throat. "Shit, that's good."

Her eyes snap to mine. "Oh. Um… good. I'm glad. I wasn't sure how you took it. Is black okay?"

I grin again. "Perfect." I take another drink, feeling the coffee flow through my veins. "Pretty sure I could live off coffee. I probably do."

She smiles softly. Butterflies I've never had suddenly take flight in my stomach. I look away and take another drink as she hugs herself. "So… uh… What… why are you here?"

"Well, something happened yesterday, Krissy. I came here to talk to you and make sure you were safe, but given what I found out, I don't blame you for not letting me in. I wasn't about to leave you alone, though."

She nods and bites her lip nervously as she looks at the ground. Her arms tighten around her midsection even tighter than they were. "Is it about Ryland Evans?"

Her voice is so low that I barely hear her. "Yeah. Yeah, it is."

She lets out a breath with another nod. Only, this one is completely defeated. She looks towards her house before glancing around her property. Finally, her eyes meet mine. "Do you want to come in? You're probably starving, and I know you can't be comfortable if you slept in your truck."

I chuckle and take another drink. "Didn't exactly sleep."

"Ugh. I feel awful. I'm so sorry, Lieutenant Andrews."

I shake my head with a grin. "Don't apologize. Trust me. I really do understand where the fear comes from." I reach for my door handle but pause. "You okay if I get out?"

She gives me another soft smile, and once again, those fucking butterflies flutter again. "I don't really know why, but I do feel like I can trust you." She steps back a couple of steps.

"You can trust me, Krissy. I know it'll take time to prove myself, but I'm not here to hurt you or fuck you up. What happened to you is… I have no words."

She nods slowly and shivers, glancing around nervously. "I'm not really doing too well out here." As if he senses it, Killer runs around the corner of the house from the backyard where he'd galavanted to. He goes right to her so she can pet him.

"He's got some good instincts on him," I comment as I slowly get out after getting my windows up. I take my keys out, my movements very deliberate. I want her to feel comfortable. "He seems very protective and in tune to you."

"Well, he's been all I've had for the past year. He's always had pretty good instincts, but the longer we're together, the better he gets at sensing things. He's gotten a lot more protective of me and doesn't let anyone near me if he doesn't trust them."

"Good. I'm glad you have him." I want to add she has me if she'll let me in, but I bite my tongue instead.

"Me too."

She starts walking to her house. I fall into step beside her but give her space. I sip my coffee and wait for her to open the door. I don't move until she looks back at me and gestures me in.

I glance around the house as I step aside so she can close and lock the door. "Really nice house. Organized."

She smiles up at me as she walks to the kitchen. "I finally have something that's mine. Really mine. I loved the free reign of decorating how I wanted."

"Modern, yet classy. Incredible art."

"I really love natural stuff. There's something so majestic about capturing flowers blowing in the wind, or a beautiful sunset or rise. I think my favorite is the dandelion." She points to a painting that's definitely the center of the room. It's hung right above the mantel.

"Wow." I walk towards it as I study it. "That's exquisite work." They caught the bend of the dandelion as the seeds blow into the wind. I almost feel like I'm there. "The colors are electric. Very vibrant. It's not subtle at all." The sun is setting in the background and casting the sky in brilliant colors. It reflects off the lake in the picture making everything so much more vibrant.

"It's so simple, yet breathtaking. Stunning."

"Who's the artist?"

"A fairly unknown artist from Minnesota. His name is James Russel, but he signs the images with JR. I have a couple of his pieces. They're equally incredible."

"You'll have to show me sometime." I turn from the picture. Krissy is getting things out of the fridge. It's hard not to look at her pretty little ass, but I force myself not to. I'd hate to embarrass her or myself if she caught me looking at her.

Krissy puts eggs, bread, bacon, and some potato rounds on the counter. She goes back to the fridge and pulls out a container with green and red peppers in it. "So, I was thinking," she begins before looking up at me. "I'm sure you want to clean up. It was hot last night, and you look like you could use a shower and some sleep."

"I know where you're going with this, and I have no intention of leaving here or sleeping until I can figure out how to keep you safe. I didn't just want to come out and say this, but he's here. Well, he's either here, or in Austin, or Waco. I don't know. He said you have contacts in both places, but he was asking about you. He came into the department asking if we'd come in contact with Phoenix Rivers. He gave me a picture of you, and he was asking around town about you."

She freezes. I can see the tears stinging her eyes. Her lip is instantly between her teeth. She bites at it nervously. I'm just about to tell her to stop when she does it on her own. "I was worried he'd find me. It was too peaceful."

"I'll stay out in my truck if that's what you want. I'll have my friend bring me some clothes and food, but I'm not leaving you unprotected until I can find someone to take over. I called my brothers, but they're with another client. Troy is on his way back, but he can't get here until tomorrow, and no one else can get here before he can."

"Your brothers?" She shakes her head. "Never mind. It's not necessary for them to come or you to stay in your truck. I called my grandparents. This place is theirs, but they've covered it well. It doesn't come back to them. It comes back to a real estate firm. My grandpa is calling a security firm he's worked with and trusts."

"What firm?" I ask.

"Prestige Guardians, I think he said."

My chest releases a little bit. "Good. That's my brother's firm. Troy, Evan, and Jason are owners." I reach for my phone when it starts ringing, and smile when I see my brother's name. "Hey, Jas," I say when I answer. "I was just talking about you."

"All great things, I hope. Look, are you at the department? I know it's the weekend, but I know you end up working overtime a lot."

"Not this weekend. Well, not with the department anyway. Something pretty big happened. I might end up taking some time off."

"Is it about Phoenix Rivers? Or Krissy Wright as she's also known? She's your neighbor, right?"

I glance at Krissy. She's busied herself with preparing the food, but I know she's listening. "Yeah. Please tell me you know that because Troy called you."

"Yeah. Don't worry. I'm on my way to your house right now. Troy wants me to stay with her until he can get here tomorrow, but I wanted to talk to you first."

"I'm with Krissy, but if you want to grab an overnight bag for me. I keep catching whiffs of myself. I slept in my truck last night, and I know I have to be grossing her out." I grin when she can't hold back a giggle.

"Yeah, I got it. How much does she know?"

"Haven't had the chance to talk to her. Long story, but she doesn't exactly trust a lot of people."

"Good to know. I'll be there in twenty."

"Kill time. Make it a couple hours. I don't want you showing up before I have the chance to talk to her."

"Fine, but keep that shit away from Troy. I don't want that fucker coming at me for not getting there as quickly as I could. If you need me, I'll be fucking up your fridge and watching a movie."

"Clothes first, asshole. Then, I don't care. Bring 'em by and get lost."

Krissy outright laughs at that. "Oh my God."

"Alright. I'll get them to you." Jason hangs up, and I chuckle.

"Sorry. That was one of my brothers."

"How many do you have?"

"Three. And they're all equally annoying as fuck and do things specifically to piss the rest of us off. Brotherly shit, you know."

"Is he coming with clothes? Because you're right. You smell awful." She doesn't turn around and look at me but does laugh with me. I take that as a sign that she trusts me. Or is at least starting to. It could be Killer laying at her feet, though.

"Should be here in about twenty minutes with that."

"Oh, thank you, Lord," she says as dramatically as I'm sure is possible.

It makes me laugh again. "I can go clean up at least. Lose the shirt. I think that's the most offensive thing on me right now."

"You really don't smell that bad. I was just teasing you." She turns to me after she gets everything into a pan. She doesn't start the burners, though. "Um... I... I'm not really good at this trusting myself thing. Everything inside me is screaming to trust you, but there's a little voice of negativity that screams even louder. And it tells me that I got in a lot of trouble when I listened to my instincts. So, I'm really trying, but I'm mostly relying on Killer and my grandparents here. If I suddenly get nervous, I'm really sorry."

"Don't be. You don't have any reason at all to be sorry, but you do have a lot of reasons to be fearful of those of us who wear a badge and carry a gun."

She sighs and looks down before seemingly putting on a brave front and looking back up at me. "I'm oddly comforted by you. That's what scares me. My automatic reaction to anyone is one laced with fear. Alarm bells are constantly ringing. With you, it's just... different. I've never had the alarm bells. I've never had bad feelings about you. That. That's what scares me. I'm more afraid that I do feel like I can trust you than I am about almost anything else. After everything that happened, I guess I just feel like I can't trust myself at all." She shakes her head and chuckles at herself. "That doesn't even make sense."

"It makes more sense than you think it does, Krissy. And I really don't blame you." I watch her eyes fall back to the counter. She plays with her fingernails as we both fall silent. After a few moments, I finally ask her something I really want to know. "Does Krissy Wright have any significance? Family? Friend? Anything?"

She shakes her head slowly. "No. I've never liked my name. I was always teased relentlessly. Ryland and his friends were always saying stuff about my name not making sense. There are no rivers in Phoenix. At least not real ones."

"Hmm. I think the Gila, Verde, and my personal favorite, the Salt, would disagree with him on that."

"That's... what I said. I didn't wake up until the next morning after that one. I earned a concussion and sprained knee for my efforts."

"Holy shit, honey. I'm sorry." I fight the urge to hug her. She looks up at me with wide eyes, and I realize what I said. "Oh. Uh. I'm sorry about that. It's a Southern thing, I think. Honey, sweetheart, ma'am. It's all kind of interchangeable with us men. I didn't mean any offense."

"No! No, it's not that. I promise. Um... it's just..." She trails off like she doesn't know how to finish her sentence even though she wants to.

"I want to know, Krissy," I say encouragingly. "Talk to me. You can be honest."

"It's nothing. I've just never really been called that before. At least not by anyone other than my grandparents." She shakes her head. "I don't have a problem with it. Anyway, you asked a question. No. There's no significance of the name. I chose it because I've always thought the last name 'Wright' was cool. And I chose 'Krissy' because it's what I've always wished I'd been named, but I never told anyone that. Not even my grandparents. I don't know anyone named Krissy."

"So, he has no idea that you like either of those names."

She shakes her head vigorously. "No. He really doesn't. No one does. I've never told anyone that. I didn't think it was important or worth mentioning. I was thinking Kira, but everyone knows my favorite Barbie is Kira. Even Ryland."

"Okay. That's really important. I don't want him finding you by looking at names he knew you liked or something."

We both look towards the door when we hear a vehicle pulling into her driveway. I take out my gun from its holster. Killer is on his feet, instantly alert.

"Caden?" Krissy whisper-shrieks.

"Get down behind the counter. Keep Killer with you." I make sure she obeys before I cautiously head for the door. I carefully peek through the crack I made in the dark brown curtain covering the small window next to the door. Jason is just getting out of his truck with a duffel bag. "Fuck," I whisper, relieved. "It's just Jason, Krissy," I call.

"Thank God."

I glance over my shoulder and see her pop up from behind the counter as I open the door. "Thanks, bro."

"You got it." He hands me the duffel bag. "Two hours, man. Troy is adamant about having someone here."

"I'm here."

He glares. "You know what I mean."

"If he has a problem, he can talk to me."

"Your ass." Jason grins and heads to his truck. "Just call when you're ready."

"I will." I close and lock the door. "You have a spare bathroom I can use?"

"There's a bathroom down here with a half shower. It's down the hall by the stairs. Otherwise, there's a spare bedroom upstairs. I've kind of turned it into my office, but the couch pulls out into a bed. Not like I have any guests."

I smile. "I won't be long. And I'm really sorry about this. I know this can't be easy."

"I've had three panic attacks in the span of twenty minutes, but I've been able to talk myself down. It'll be okay. I'm really trying."

I give her a soft smile. "I know it doesn't mean much without proof to back up the words, but you can trust me. I just want to help and keep you safe."

She nods. "I know."

"If you need me -"

"I'll run screaming for you." She gives me a teasing smile, but I can see that she's very much serious.

It's my turn to nod. "Good. Do that."

I head for the shower down here just so she doesn't have to run far if she does need me.

I pray she doesn't.

Chapter Five

♡ Krissy ♡

I finish putting the last dish away after I dry it. Caden insisted on doing them when we finished breakfast. He wouldn't take no for an answer, and I was quite taken aback. My grandpa does that for my grandma, but I always thought they just had a unique relationship. I didn't grow up with parents who did that. My mother did the housework. My dad worked.

"Ready to talk now?" Caden is leaning against the counter near the sink.

I sigh. "I guess. There's no way around it, is there?"

"You could tell me to go fuck myself. Wouldn't be able to help you then, though."

I nibble my lip and wrap my sweater around me. It's hot outside, but I have central air. It's nice and cool in here, but right now, it's too cold. I walk to the living room. Killer is curled up in his large dog bed near the window. He loves to bask in the sunlight and nap. I love that he's near when I'm lounging.

I sit down on my beige sectional couch. It matches the gorgeous hardwood floors and beautiful dark brown rug I have in this room. It brightens everything up while still matching the theme. My grandparents wanted a cabin on the lake feel. I've always thought they succeeded perfectly with this house.

Caden chooses one of my comfy, oversized chairs that faces the couch. I can't help but notice that he hasn't gotten close. He's allowed me to decide the distance between us. No other man has ever been that considerate.

"Where do I even start?" I ask as I play with the end of the blanket.

"How about your real name?"

I chuckle. "Phoenix Rivers. But you knew that."

"I did, but best to confirm it all, right? Big difference between thinking I'm right and knowing I am."

"I suppose that's true." I don't look up. I need him to guide me because I really don't know how to explain everything. Specific questions to answer would be helpful.

"Good start. I did read over reports and stuff. I know you filed assault and sexual assault charges that he was convicted of. A few others were convicted of sexual assault. It gives some pretty gruesome details."

"I was gang raped. I was drugged. I don't remember a lot of it. Some comes back, but it's all very fuzzy. I know there were three other people. There may have been more, but I only remember three plus him. So four. Ryland was holding me down for a lot of it, but he had his turn, too. The only reason I was able to get the other three convicted of that with him is because I did remember enough details to convince the judge. They all waived their right to a jury. They didn't think the judge would take my word over that of cops. I was able to identify certain features of each person's private area. When they first started, I wasn't totally out of it. That's how I'm certain there were three friends and him. When I woke up from that, I was in the psych ward at the hospital. His brother was my doctor and somehow found a way to keep me there for ninety-eight days before my grandparents were able to get me out."

"Tell me about how this all started. How did you meet this asshole?"

I chuckle again, only this time it's dark and wry. "It would be a cute meet-cute if things didn't go as they did. It was a traffic stop. My taillights were out. I didn't know. He stopped me and let me know. Then, he offered to take a look at them himself. He was really sweet. He followed me home. We exchanged numbers. He came the very next day and fixed them himself really fast. And then took me to dinner. Looking back, the trouble started right away, but it was super subtle. I like my steak rare. He made me feel guilty about ordering it rare and convinced me to order it medium well, but it was so sweet and subtle that I didn't even realize it happened. Then, it went to clothes. He didn't like what I wore to bed, which was really what I am now. Just no sweater."

"Tank top and shorts?"

"Mmhmm. He made me wear a t-shirt and sleep pants. But again, it was subtle. He didn't just come out and say he didn't like it. He bought me pajamas and was happy when he saw me in them. Then, it went to my clothes in general. He'd just buy stuff he liked until I was dressing how he wanted. He never really said anything about the clothes I was wearing until later on. He went through all my stuff and put them in a donation box. I came home from work when he was putting everything in his car. This was months after. I didn't know what it was at first, but later that night, after he left, I went to change and noticed that all of my old, comfortable stuff was gone. I still wore some of the stuff when he wasn't around just when I wanted to watch a movie."

"So, he started manipulating you."

"Yeah, but I didn't know it was happening. When I asked him about the stuff, he just said that it was stuff that made me look fat. Now, I had clothes that flattered me, but he threw in a dig. It was the first time he did it, but I felt very self-conscious right away. He said the clothes flattered me and also hid my flaws, like my fat thighs. Not long after that, he was dragging me to the gym every day. If he came over when I was binging a movie series or something and eating anything he considered junk food, he'd berate me until I felt bad about it. I changed my entire diet around and lost a lot of weight. Then, he'd berate me for having lost too much and not eating right."

"Christ."

"Oh…, it gets worse," I whisper. Little flashes of things that happened play through my mind like a movie. "The first time he hit me was over something so stupid. I moved in with him, and I came home from work dog tired and so stressed. I just wanted to go to sleep. I thought he worked night shift, but he was working a day shift. When he got home, I was passed out in bed. I didn't cook anything. I just laid down and went to sleep. I woke up to him pulling me out of bed and calling me lazy. He was screaming at me about dinner. The first mistake was going to sleep. The second was suggesting we get takeout. It set him off like a bomb. He detonated and left me one hell of a mess. I couldn't go to work for a week, and when I did, I had to use heavy makeup. Everyone could see right through it since I don't wear a lot to begin with."

"Did you file a report?"

I shake my head. "No. He made it very clear no one would believe me. And I believed him. Especially since by that time, he'd killed my self-esteem. There were several more beatings. One of them sent me to the hospital, and the nurse reported it. The problem was the person who took the report was one of his close friends."

"So, the report never made it far."

I shake my head. "Nope. It basically just said it was a dispute between us with a lot of yelling. No mention of my injuries. No images. No arrests. It went on like that for a while, and each time someone reported it, it wasn't me who did it. It was a coworker, usually. I'd get another beating because of the report. My family believed everything he said. Except my grandparents. They couldn't prove anything, but they knew something wasn't right. I lied a lot because I thought it was the only way to save my life. I remember every little thing that happened. I remember the good times and bad. I still have horrible nightmares. I have severe PTSD from it. Loud noises? I don't do well with them. Yelling? I sometimes end up catatonic. I actually ended up getting away from him, thanks to my grandparents, but he found me."

"What happened with that?"

"That was the gang rape. He showed up at the small apartment I was able to rent with my grandparent's help. Everything was in my name. He'd never met them. He always avoided it for some reason. I think it's because everyone else thought he was amazing. He didn't think he needed to meet anyone else to convince them he was so great. And I really never wanted him to meet them. I wanted to selfishly keep them to myself. I didn't want him to turn them. Anyway, he showed up, forced his way in. At first, it was okay. He was just talking. He was being genuine. Apologizing. It wasn't really fooling me, but when he offered me a drink, I didn't think anything of it. He was a lot of things, but he'd never tried to drug me."

"He did that night, though."

"Yep. I was groggy but still alert when he brought his friends in. I vividly remember three of them being there with him. They had their way with me. I could feel everything, but I was going more and more under because of the drugs. They were still going at it when I completely passed out. When I woke the next morning, I was in the hospital. I was barely out of the fog when I was being taken somewhere else. By the time I was fully awake and alert, I found out I'd been committed to the psych ward at the hospital. I wasn't allowed to make any phone calls. I wasn't allowed to contact anyone. The more I argued, the worse it got for me. I was restrained. Sedated. The first couple of weeks are an absolute blur. Every time I seemed to come back to myself, I was sedated again. After the third week, the drugs came less and less. By the fourth week, I finally saw my doctor."

"His brother?"

"You guessed it." I shrug. "I think I already knew, but it was confirmed then. It became an entirely different fight, though. It became a fight for freedom and survival, and it had to be tactful and well-planned. So, I spent my days figuring out what I needed to do to get out. I learned when they asked questions about things, like what happened in my relationship with Ryland, if I told the truth, it was another sedation. If I talked about the rape, same thing. By the tenth week, I learned to lie and be really good at it. The twelfth week, I got a surprise. A lawyer came to visit me. I told him literally everything, including what had been happening in the facility."

"Your grandparents hired him?"

"I found that out later. The lawyer was a friend of theirs. He left them completely out of it. As far as anyone was concerned, he took the case pro bono. I'm not even sure that wasn't the truth. I don't know if my grandparents paid him or not. But he was there. He took my case. And I got sedated the second he left. I'm pretty sure I stayed in a vegetative state for a while because there are about three weeks that I really don't remember anything about. Just blurs. Like smelling something really bad and being bathed and changed and put back into bed. My lawyer brought three trials to court. The first was the abuse. After the first couple of times, I got smart and started taking pictures. I saved them to my phone in a hidden folder that I archived. The second was the gang rape. The third was against his brother for holding me against my will."

"The results I found are that he was found guilty of the abuse and rape. His friends were, too. And I didn't find anything on the brother."

"You probably wouldn't have. It's not public record. He managed to get that sealed. He wasn't found guilty. It came out in court that my parents had a hand in getting me committed. They managed to get some kind of temporary guardianship over me based on lie after lie that I couldn't disprove at the time because I had no idea they were behind anything. When it was all over, all I had was my grandparents and Killer, the dog they bought for me just before I got my apartment. I was waiting on my landlord to approve my dog, so he was staying with my grandparents at the time I was there. Ryland and his buddies all got five years in jail and had to register as sexual predators. He's not supposed to be out yet."

"Good behavior," Caden says. "I looked into it. He worked the entire time. That gave him an opportunity to claim two days served for every day he served. He basically cut his sentence in half and ended up on parole for the rest of his sentence, which is two more years, from what I gathered."

"Yeah." For the first time, I look up at him. Caden has his gunbelt on, but I'm not nervous at all.

Something about him makes me feel like I can trust him. He's exactly the opposite of Ryland in every aspect. He exudes confidence, kindness, and compassion. All I ever got from Ryland was cockiness. Even at the beginning, something threw me about him, but I ignored it completely. That was a huge mistake. One that nearly cost me my life. One that gave me such severe trauma and trust issues, I doubt I'll ever truly recover.

Caden, though. He's real. Genuine. The differences are so obvious that it's comical I could've ever been so stupid when it came to Ryland. So fucking stupid. Blinded by a hot guy who was interested in the likes of me. I've always been a simple soul. I don't need much to make me happy, and I never felt the need to try hard to convince someone to like me. I figured if they didn't like me for the person I am, then they don't deserve to have me in their life.

Ryland somehow managed to make me flip all of that on its head. Suddenly, all I wanted to do was whatever he wanted me to as long as it made him happy. Even if it meant quitting my job and turning myself into an entirely different person.

So stupid.

"Still with me?" Caden's deep voice cuts through my thoughts, and I shake myself out of my thoughts.

"Yeah. I am. Sorry. Just got lost."

"Well, I won't let you get lost. I'm right here. Do you need anything? My brother should be here soon. Do you want some water? Might give you a chance to relax before he comes over. Troy is on his way. He should be here tomorrow. In the meantime, Jason is going to stay with you."

I nod. I can't say I'm not disappointed. I hoped Caden would stay. I'm trusting him more and more the longer I spend with him. Killer is comfortable with him. I don't want to meet anyone else and have a stranger staying with me. Caden isn't necessarily a stranger to me. I've seen him around. He's talked to me a few times, even if I have practically run back into my house.

"An ice water would be nice."

"Comin' up, darlin'," he drawls with a wink.

What that does to my insides is something I'll have to keep to myself, but it comes as a total shock. No one, not even Ryland, has ever had that kind of effect on me. Especially with just three words. Hell, his deep Southern accent could kill me, and I'd die a happy woman.

As I wait for him to come back, I can't help but continuously think how different he is. He's nothing like Ryland. He's protective and kind. He's caring and understanding. He's empathetic. When he was asking me questions, I felt like I really wanted to tell him. I didn't feel like he was forcing information out of me like other police officers I've dealt with, especially Ryland.

I've allowed myself to indulge in fantasies of Caden, but I've never gone further than that. I've done everything to keep him at a distance despite the war in my mind that tells me to trust him and not to. It's like I'm two people. One side really wants to move on from everything and not live in fear anymore. To start trusting people again. The other side wants to stay hidden. Be alone. No one can hurt me if I'm alone.

It's a battle with myself. I'm not sure if there can be a winner or loser when there's so much at stake.

When I look at him, though, everything changes. He's a force of nature. Calm yet fierce. Soothing yet dangerous. I feel deep down I could let my guard down with him.

I just don't trust myself not to lead me astray…

Chapter Six

♡ Caden ♡

(One Week Later)

"Did you say you were upside down?" one of our younger female dispatchers asks in disbelief as she furiously types. I set some coffee and a donut down next to her as I pause. "Yes, sir. It's okay. I have rescue already on their way to you. Can you just stay on the line for me?"

I take a glance at the screen. It looks to be on the highway on the outskirts of town heading to Austin. The kid is young. Nineteen. I know the name well enough to know I've stopped him for speeding more times than I can count. I walk towards our other dispatcher answering calls today.

"No response. The call came in from Life Alert," the other dispatcher says. He's an older guy, but not too much. He's in forties. Retired military who just wanted to feel like he's still helping people. Shane is his name.

I set a coffee and donut next to him. The call is about an older lady. There ain't many details. Just her name and address. Call notes say the call came in from Life Alert. They say she'd pushed the button, but they can't get ahold of her to get more details. Shane has already sent out rescue to her.

I walk back to our female dispatcher, Annie, who seems to be getting a little flustered. "Yes, sir, I understand. Rescue is almost there. Let's just take a few deep breaths together."

"Put me on that call," I say low enough for only her to hear.

She nods and gives me a grateful smile as she mouths the words 'thank you'. I grin and wink, hoping it calms her slightly. I give her shoulder a squeeze as I head out after I finish passing out the rest of the donuts I have with coffee. We don't have a giant dispatcher center, only about three or four people working at one time, but I like bringing in treats for them. They work hard and need to feel appreciated.

I stride through the bullpen and past the locker rooms to the garage. I jump in my squad after a quick safety check and drive out of the garage towards Highway 183. I turn on my lights and sirens so I can maneuver easily through the busy Friday traffic. The nice thing about a small town is even if it's busy, it's not so busy that it makes it impossible to get places. Traffic jams are rare, and everyone is very good at moving over for emergency vehicles.

Of course, we still get our nosy neighbors. The ones who look out their window at everything going on, or are far less subtle and just walk outside to watch. Every small town has someone who's the town gossip, and someone else who knows everyone and everything.

I turn onto the highway and sigh at all the slowed down traffic as I look down at my laptop for the call details. I make my way down the shoulder of the highway being very cautious of anyone who might try to be an idiot and cut me off. I never trust other drivers not to panic and do something they wouldn't otherwise do. Like hear my sirens and try to get out of the way by turning right into me.

The call details say it's a three car crash. Fire and an ambulance were already dispatched and are probably there already. It looks like another squad was also already dispatched and someone from the State Patrol is probably already here, too. I really don't need to be here, but I'm fucking bored and need to take my mind off Krissy.

When I pull up to the accident, I'm not at all surprised to see Officer Tate Channing already out directing traffic. What I am surprised to see is no other squads from County or State. I quickly grab the mic I picked up on my way out and hook it up to my radio. I get out of my squad and walk briskly to the trunk to grab my neon green traffic vest.

After I get the vest on, I clip the mic to my shoulder. "Squad Four to radio," I say into my keyed mic.

"Squad Four? Go ahead," dispatch answers.

"I'm two-three. Can we get State out here?"

"Squad Four is two-three at fifteen-thirty-eight. State is Code Three. ETA fifteen minutes."

"Ten-four." I walk towards Tate.

"Man, am I happy to see you," he says, sweat beading from his brow and dripping from his forehead. "It's fucking hot out here."

"Go grab some water. Cool down. It's over a hundred right now. Grab your water and go sit in my squad. It's cool." I hand him my keys.

"Thanks, Lieutenant." Tate takes the keys and quickly walks to his squad. He ducks inside and grabs his drink before quickly heading to my squad. He could sit in his, but his is blocking traffic. I don't want him in his squad just in case someone hits it. He could get hurt.

I focus on the traffic and keep it moving by letting people in the left lane go for a while before I stop it. I wave the people in the right lane into the left and let them go for a while before I do the same thing and stop them. I switch between the two lines until I see a tow truck making its way down the shoulder.

There are two cars in the ditch and a pickup truck blocking the right lane. It'a miracle more vehicles weren't involved in this mess, but I'm grateful not to see more destruction.

Tate sees the tow truck and gets out of my squad. "What do you need, Andrews? Tow truck is coming."

"I don't see State yet. Block off the left lane for me. I'm gonna let these guys go and stop them further back so the tow truck can get by."

"You got it." Tate stops the left lane. I let the right lane go and keep waving them by as I walk up the shoulder a few car lengths back. I let a few more go before I stop them again.

"Squad Thirty-Four," I say into my mic. "Let them go. Walk up the lane towards me. We'll stop them up here so the tow can get by."

"Ten-four." Tate follows my commands. We let a few cars go by before we stop everyone again.

"Thanks, guys. Appreciate you," the tow truck driver, an older man who's a little overweight and graying says. "Got a couple more on the way."

I nod. "We'll let 'em through." I wipe my forehead and see a couple motorcycles a few cars back. It's dangerous for them to be in traffic jams. If someone doesn't see the traffic stopped and causes a larger accident, people on bikes can get seriously hurt or even be killed. "Tate, I'm gonna let these bikes go, man. I want them outta here."

"Good idea."

I start walking towards the bikes. "Hey, guys. Let's get you outta here," I say when I reach them.

"Wouldn't mind that, Officer!" one of them says. He's got a girl on the back of his bike, as do the others.

"You guys just out for a ride?"

"Yes, sir. Didn't expect an accident. Hope everyone's okay."

"Haven't heard anything that leads me to believe they ain't, but I hope so, too. Watch yourselves, but follow me through here."

"Yes, sir."

I start walking back up the line with the bikers following, walking their bikes behind me, though they're still on them. Once we reach the front, the tow truck is already pulled ahead of the accident. He can't do anything until accident investigation gets here, which is State Patrol.

I lead them towards Tate's squad before pointing down the road and turning to them. "Stay on the left hand shoulder. Watch the glass and debris. The truck's bumper is in the middle of the road on the other side of the squad."

"Thank you, sir. Appreciate you very much."

"You're welcome. Ya'll drive safe."

They all give nods as they take off slowly until they clear the scene. I walk back towards the line of traffic. I see lights and hear sirens in the distance, so I decide to let more traffic go until State is on scene.

Once they do arrive, we shut down the traffic movement until he's able to get pictures and measurements. He does it as quickly as he can and allows us to get more traffic flowing.

What seems like hours pass. Tate and I have both needed water breaks and taken them as we've been able to. Even the fire department has taken turns sitting in the truck and getting water.

"Hey, man," Blake Falcon, Captain of the fire crew on shift today, says. He's tall, muscular, and tattooed, just as I am. We've been friends awhile and are big fans of the Guns and Hoses baseball game that happens for charity every year. We might be friends, but we're even better rivals.

"Hey. How's it going?"

"Nineteen-year-old is drunk and dumb. He was going way too fucking fast. Hit a Toyota with a couple girls in it who were heading to Austin for some shopping. Girls are okay. Scratches. Thank fuck they were wearing their seatbelts. The Chevy truck hit the girls after the kid hit them. Chevy caused the Toyota to spin. Then, the Chevy hit the kid while the kid was spinning. The Chevy had a father with his three-year-old in there. Both are okay. He has some scratches, but the kid doesn't have any bumps or bruises at all. The drunk kid, though. He's another story. He's not severely hurt, I don't think. Might have some internal damage, but he's got one hell of a concussion."

I sigh and rub my head. "I've stopped that kid many times for speeding. I told him the next time I saw him, he'd get it for reckless driving and lose his fucking license. Never caught him drinking, though."

"Yeah, we got him out. He's pretty okay, surprisingly, considering the state of his car. He flipped a few times. We had to cut him out. State is running a breathalyzer on him, but he reeked of booze and weed."

I roll my eyes. "Lethal combination. And look what could've happened if just one variable had changed. He could've killed people today."

"Well, you must've had a lasting impression on the kid because he kept saying not to tell Lieutenant Andrews. Didn't care about his parents. Just you."

"Fuck me." I sigh and shake my head before turning back to Tate. "You got this?"

"Yeah, I'm good."

I follow Blake towards the ambulance where State is giving the kid a breathalyzer. The tow trucks are clearing the cars off the road. I sigh again. "Jimothy, come on. What're you doing, man?"

Jimothy is sitting on the back of the ambulance. He looks up at me teary. "Fuck, Lieutenant. I fucked up, okay? I was pissed and wasn't thinkin'."

"That's obvious. Think about what could've happened here. You could've killed people."

"It's just my parents. They took off on another fuckin' cruise with my little brother."

"And left you again?" I raise an eyebrow.

"Yeah," he grumbles. "Didn't even leave money for food and there's nothing in the fridge. They emptied it before they left."

"What did you blow?"

"He blew a point five, sir," the Trooper says to me. "We were gonna get a draw from him. He said he smoked some weed, too."

"Only one joint, man. That's not why I crashed. I was speeding and lost control. I told you that."

"Squad Four. Wife of the truck is here," Tate says over the radio. "Also, looks like someone else is arriving."

"Probably for the girls. Let them both through. Tell them to park next to fire."

"Ten-four."

"Do you have their statements? Or do you need me to help out?" I ask the Trooper.

"Nah. They're good to go. I got 'em."

"Go release them. Get them outta here, then come back here. We can talk about what to do with Jimothy."

"Yes, sir."

I scrub a hand down my face before looking back at Jimothy as the Trooper walks away. "What the fuck, man? What the hell happened to college? You should be outta here by now."

Jimothy looks up at me. "I never got the acceptance letter, man. I found out my parents got into my email and deleted them. They watched the mail and took the acceptance packages and everything. They keep telling me not to waste my time or their money. I'm not smart enough to make it."

I sit next to him and sigh. "Look, Jimothy. I don't know if I can get you out of this. You're legally below the legal limit, but you admitted to speeding and driving under the influence. He can get you for reckless driving, I'm sure. It's his scene. It doesn't matter how lenient I choose to be with you or my rank. As soon as they get all the shit put together with the investigation, you could get endangerment, and a lot of other shit.

You're likely to get fines up the ass for this, at the very least. Probably jail time."

Jimothy drops his head. "I fucked everything up. I know. I usually do."

"I don't know, man. I don't know how bad this is for you, yet. Maybe we can call the colleges still and -"

"I already tried, Lieutenant. It's no use. My parents fucked that up, and then I fucked my entire life up. Just give up on me."

"That's not happening," the Trooper says, reappearing. "No one is giving up on anyone. Look, preliminary investigation says to me that it's your fault. You were speeding. You admitted that. But I didn't hear anything about alcohol or weed."

Both of us snap our eyes to him. I immediately start searching for a bodycam, but I don't see one. I have one, but I shut it off on my way over here. "What are you talking about?" I ask.

"Yeah, you clearly said -"

The Trooper cuts Jimothy off. "I clearly said you need to drive more careful, kid." He tilts his head to me and walks away.

I follow him after giving Jimothy a 'wait a minute' look. "What's going on?" I ask him once we're a fair distance away from everyone. The last tow truck is driving away.

"Remember that BOLO you put out about Ryland Evans?" he asks.

"Yeah…," I say with narrowed, suspicious eyes as I fold my arms over my chest.

"Well, I was just dealing with him near Waco. He came into our office asking some questions. We arrested him and are going to ship his ass back to Minnesota. That's what tied me up getting here, but here's the deal. I just got a call after I released the other accident victims from one of my coworkers. Evans was talking about Jimothy. Used his name specifically. He was looking for him. Said he was a contact of the girl he's after. Phoenix Rivers."

"Jimothy Rivers…," I mumble, trying to connect the dots. "Where are you going with this?"

"He said he's this girl's son."

"That's not possible. She'd have been eight when she had him."

"That's what I said. When he was talking to me, what he told me about the girl is minimal, but he did mention her age. Twenty-six. Now, he's saying she's lying about it."

"No. That's not fucking possible. I did a lot of research after that. I ran her. She's twenty-six." I don't tell him that I've talked to her grandparents. I don't tell him that the security company hired to protect her is owned by my brothers.

"I know. I know, man. I'm just letting you know. I don't know what the fuck is going on, but whatever it is, he's after that girl and looking for Jimothy, too."

"Thanks for letting me know." I pat his shoulder as we head back to Jimothy.

"Take care of him, man. Get him the fuck out of here because everything about that interaction is fucking with my head. Add on this call, and I don't like this one bit. He's in your jurisdiction. My hands are tied unless you tell me specifically to take the case."

"I'll get him somewhere safe."

"The reason I'm bringing this up is because I was going to let him go after I got that call. The problem is I don't want to let him go if he has no place to really go to. It doesn't look like he has a lot of people he can trust, from what I heard. Looks like he trusts you."

"He's had a rough life. I've been both hard on him and done a lot to help him out. Maybe this is what we need to get him out of the situation he's in. I've only been able to do so much. I told him the last time I dealt with him that he needed to start acting more responsible, or I'd get him for reckless driving and take his license, but he knows as well as I do, I'd never do that. Too much would be at stake if I had."

After we clear the scene, I get in my squad car. Jimothy is in the front passenger's seat. He's quiet and wringing his hands together. I've already put in a call to Troy. He's going to have one of his guys meet me at my house to bring Jimothy to a safehouse. From there, we can figure all of this out while keeping him safe.

And while that's happening, hopefully Krissy will be able to give some insight on who this kid is to her. It seems odd that Ryland would pull some random kid out of a hat and connect him to her.

Over the past week, Krissy has been opening up and trusting me more and more. She's getting along well with Troy, who is her full-time bodyguard. I've seen her almost every night. I've even stayed with her most nights. The two nights I didn't see her, we talked on the phone. I like her more every time we talk, but I love that she trusts me enough to allow me to stay with her instead of my brother.

I glance at the clock on my dashboard and choke down the sigh. It's almost eight at night. I'm starving. I'm sure Jimothy is. I still have some paperwork to do. There's no way I'm getting out of here anytime soon, so I decide to order dinner for me and Jimothy and have Troy's guy meet us at the department while I finish up the shit I need to do.

And as soon as Jimothy is safe, my next call will be to Krissy. Not only do I miss her, something I'm completely shocked about because I've never really liked a woman enough to miss her, but I really just want to hear her voice.

She's becoming the light in my dark world.

Chapter Seven

♡ Krissy ♡

I smile up at Caden after the movie we were just watching ends. "I really love *Two Weeks Notice*. It's one of the greats."

He gives me a soft smile, but his eyes are far away. They've been that way ever since he got here. He was over five hours late, though. He didn't say much. Just that he got tied up on a call. One of the things I learned from Ryland was to not ask about his job. Not only did he not like questions, but he really didn't like when the questions were asked about his job. At first, he told me he didn't like bringing work home with him. That made sense, and I understood.

But sometimes, he was so upset that it pulled at my heartstrings. I felt so bad for him sometimes that while I didn't ask him details or anything, I would try and let him know that I was there for him. He could talk if he wanted to.

The more I cared, though, the more violent he got with me. Eventually, it wasn't just him telling me to shut up. He wasn't just screaming at me. He was holding me over the sink with the water running over my face. Or he'd hold my hand over the garbage disposal and threaten to put it in there, *Kingpin* style. I stopped asking because I didn't want to die. I didn't want to be beaten to death. I started doing a lot of things to avoid what he'd do to me. Anything to keep him from hitting me.

I look back at the TV, but I feel myself becoming more and more timid. Caden's arm is around me, and I'm snuggled into his side. We're both cuddled into a blanket. Caden had eaten at his office a while ago, but I made a chicken salad. He was a little hungry when he got here, and I'd kept some in the fridge for him just in case. It's been so hot this summer that the thought of turning on the oven makes me want to throw up, so I opted for something cold and easy.

"Want to watch another movie?" I ask, trying to cut through the tension I feel. It's after midnight, but he doesn't have to work tomorrow, and I'm too tense to sleep. Killer is lying under the coffee table at our feet. His ears perk up, but he doesn't move.

"Yeah. You got any popcorn and trail mix?"

I furrow my brows and tilt my head. "Um… I think I might, actually. Troy seems to love trail mix."

"All of us Andrews brothers do." Caden grins as he starts to get up. Killer chooses then to move. He bounds to the back door, expecting to go outside. Caden obliges him before finding my popcorn and snack stash. He knows it's in the pantry near the refrigerator.

"Do you need any help?" I ask as I get up and walk slowly towards him. I sense something is wrong, but I'm really afraid to ask. We've been in some kind of friendly relationship for a little while now, but I don't trust myself, or anyone else, fully. I'm expecting him to turn on me like Ryland did.

He sighs but says nothing. I approach him cautiously, but keep my distance as he puts a bag of popcorn in the microwave. Once he sets the time, he turns towards me quickly. I flinch, wince, and shrink back, bracing for a hit.

"Hey, sweetheart," Caden says soothingly. He stays where he is with his hands at his sides. "What just happened, Krissy?" His voice reverberates through me, calming me in ways I've never been before. My racing heart begins to slow almost before it reaches an unhealthy level of beating.

I look up at him, biting my lip. I'm not to the point where I can speak, but I need to see him. I need to know he's not going to hurt me. Not going to slap me so hard, I fall down stairs. Caden looks at me with nothing but concern and confusion, but there's one thing that shines through it all.

Protection.

He looks like he'll throw whatever or whoever caused this reaction in me to the most vicious of all predators and watch as they eat the cause of all of this alive.

My body is still tense, but his slow movements help. He keeps his eyes on me as he takes the bag of popcorn out of the microwave when it's done.

"Take a deep breath, darlin'," he rumbles. I do it because his tone, dominant, yet smooth, leaves me no other choice.

And I need that. I need him to lead me. It's something I've always needed. Something Ryland never gave me. At least not the healthy way.

Caden watches me while he mixes the trail mix into the popcorn. I'm still not quite able to talk. I'm fighting off memories and convincing myself he's not going to hit me. Caden pops an M&M in his mouth after he's mixed the popcorn and trail mix.

"Another deep breath, Krissy. You're still not there. Come on. One more for me."

I keep doing as he says. I keep my attention solely on him and my breathing. Despite the fact that his sudden movement sent me into this state, he's also the only one who can bring me out of it so quickly. I realize each and every single day that I really do trust him.

After a few more moments of breathing, I allow my eyes to close briefly. I open them slowly and focus on him once more. He's leaning against the counter.

"Talk to me, beautiful. What happened? What did I do?"

I shake my head and blink a few times. "It's... not your fault."

"Then, tell me what happened, so I can be better prepared in the future. I know whatever just happened has to do with PTSD. I'm not an expert, but I know the signs when I see them."

I let out a long breath and look down. "It's just that... you've been quiet... I know from experience that probably means you had a long day or a bad day. I know cops don't like bringing work home, but sometimes, I feel like they leave it all inside when they shouldn't. I wanted to ask if everything was okay, but I learned quickly not to do that."

"He'd hit you."

I nod. "I learned to not ask, even if I wanted to. But sometimes, not even that worked. He'd just be in a bad mood and take it out on me... You moved fast... That's all."

Caden holds out his hand. He doesn't step towards me. He leaves the choice to me. I'm sure he knows exactly what he's doing, and I've never been so grateful to anyone for anything. I haven't had very many choices I've gotten to make in a long time. Usually, they've been made for me. Not a lead, but a demand. Coming here, to Piper Falls, wasn't really even my choice. It was done out of necessity.

Not that I don't like it here. I'm even starting to love it.

Or maybe it's just someone...

I take Caden's hand, and he closes his around mine. His large hand engulfs mine, but it's not even close to where my focus is. The spark I feel every time my skin touches his sends bumps all over my body. I could melt into him if I let myself.

His thumb rubs light circles over the back of my hand. "I'm not going to hurt you. I hate everything he did to you. I would really like nothing more than to fuck him up for that." He tugs my hand just enough for me to know he wants me to step closer to him.

I do without hesitation, and that surprises me, but comforts me all the same.

When I'm in front of him, his other hand snakes around my waist. He moves slow, but deliberately. I know what he wants. He's taking what he wants. But he's giving me the opportunity to pull away.

I don't.

In fact, I step even closer, but I have no control over the action. My body is the one leading now. Caden wraps both arms around me and pulls me flush against his chest while still leaving every opportunity for me to run. Our eyes meet and fire explodes between us like an inferno.

"Tell me you understand," he rumbles, barely above a whisper. His voice is like satin washing over me.

"I understand," I whisper. My eyes drop to his lips. I want him to kiss me so badly. I didn't realize it until right this moment. Not that I haven't thought of what it would be like. I have. A lot. But I've always fought it away.

I don't want to fight it anymore.

He leans his closer, his lips just brushing mine, when Killer barks at the back door. I jump, but Caden holds me closer as he chuckles and glances at the door. His eyes fall back on me. "Cockblocked."

I can't help the giggle that escapes my throat as I step away. "I'll get drinks and bring your popcorn concoction to the table."

"It's the best. You'll love it." He heads for the door as I open the fridge to grab some iced tea for us. "I will have that kiss," he says as he lets Killer in.

My face heats up as he locks the door. "Looking forward to it," I say so quietly, I'm sure he doesn't hear me.

I feel his hand drop to my waist as I stand with the pitcher of tea in my hand. "Good," he rumbles against my neck right before he kisses it. I feel my knees get weak as he steps away. So much for him not hearing me. He grabs two glasses as I grip the counter and cross my legs to keep what he does to me at bay.

He chuckles as he sets the cups down. "I got the popcorn." He picks up the bowl and strolls to the living room like he didn't just cause me to nearly make an embarrassing mess in my short jean shorts.

I follow behind him with our drinks. We settle as he finds another movie. Once we settle on *A Day After Tomorrow*, we both get comfortable again. Once again, in his arms, I feel the safest I've ever felt. I could really get used to this. It both terrifies me and makes me excited for what the future could possibly hold.

Once we're settled, it takes all of ten seconds for Caden's lips to meet mine in a kiss capable of making the world simply explode. When his tongue touches mine, I see stars. My eyes feel so heavy with lust, I couldn't open them if I tried. Instead, I allow him to completely control the kiss and the pace of it.

His tongue swipes across mine. He tastes like coffee and sin. As I sink deeper into him, I realize that not only is he in complete control, but I love it. I trust it.

I trust him.

His fingertips tangle in my hair as he grips the back of my neck. He angles his head in such a way that it allows him to dominate me even more, but the best thing is that while he has all of the control, he's reading me. He's not taking more than I'm willing to give. His pace isn't too much for me. It's perfect.

He's so perfect. I want to cry.

When he pulls away slowly, it takes everything in me not to crawl into his lap and beg for more. I stay rooted to my spot staring into the deep depths of the first man who has ever made me feel those proverbial butterflies.

"You can always ask me how my day was. I'm not going to get upset with you. If I have a bad day, I'm not ever taking that out on you. Understand?" He never takes his eyes off me.

I nod slowly, still trying to come back down from the high he sent me to. I realize I'm gripping his massive, muscular arm, so I focus on his tattoos as I clear my throat. "I understand," I whisper.

He tilts my jaw up with his index finger so I'm looking at him. "Look at me, baby. Tell me you understand."

The softness of his commanding tone does something to my insides. It's everything I've ever needed and more. "Yes, sir. I understand," I say a little more confidently. I watch his Adam's apple bob as he swallows. His eyes appear to be on fire, and I realize all at once what calling him 'sir' does to him.

"Good girl," he rumbles low, almost like a growl as he trails his hand down my arm.

And that's when it happens.

My eyes roll back in my head. My pussy muscles clench. My stomach tightens. I bite my lip to stop the scream as waves upon waves of pleasure crash over me. I grip his shirt even tighter and barely am aware that he's watching every second of what's happening to me.

When it's over and I'm coming down, legs clenched together tight, my cheeks heat and turn an unnatural shade of bright red. I let go of his shirt quickly, like it burned me. "Oh God," I whisper under my breath.

His grin turns into a smirk so fast, it makes my head spin. He squeezes my upper thigh, and I can't stop the gasp the simple motion elicits. He leans in so close, his lips brush mine. "If I can make you come without actually trying, imagine how good it'll feel when I do it on purpose."

I bite my lip as I get up. "I should… probably… um… bed. I should sleep." I stand awkwardly in front of him.

He looks me up and down like he wants to devour me. I'd let him if he asked, and that scares me. I barely know him.

"Okay. Sweet dreams, sweet girl." He leans back on the couch, but he never stops undressing me with his eyes. I scurry upstairs and don't breathe until my door is safely closed behind me.

I hadn't realized that Killer followed me, but I shouldn't be surprised. It's become our routine. If he hadn't followed me is when I think I would've noticed.

Like he usually does, he jumps onto my bed as I hurry to the bathroom to clean up. Once I finish, I crawl into bed with just a tank top and panties. Killer is already fast asleep and barely moves when he feels me. He just huffs out a breath like he's annoyed I dare disturb his slumber. It makes me giggle until I start imagining it's Caden lying there instead.

Caden has been sleeping in the guest bedroom like the perfect gentleman. When he's gone, Troy, one of Caden's brothers, has been here. He doesn't leave until Caden is inside with me with the doors locked. I love that Caden is here almost every night. His brother is great, but I always feel safer with Caden.

I'm relaxed with him near.

I'm not sure if I'm falling in love or if I'm already there, but fuck it if I can't have us.

He's all I want.

Chapter Eight

♡ Caden ♡

"Rrrrr…," I groan as I reach for my cellphone to shut off my fucking alarm. The second I have it off, it goes off again, and I realize someone is actually calling me. I don't bother to look at the caller ID. "Someone better be dead," I growl into the phone.

A chuckle followed by a yawn. "You owe me your first born for what I'm about to tell you."

I raise an eyebrow as I look at the clock on the nightstand. "Mateo? It's three in the morning. What the fuck are you doing up?"

"Got a call from my Captain. Preston just put me on Jimothy's case."

"At three in the morning?"

"Yep. Turns out he got a call from your Captain. Guess who woke Laura up?"

I sigh and sit up knowing I'm not getting any more sleep. "Who?"

"Ryland fucking Evans. From the county fucking jail in Wako."

My mind is spinning with questions I can't ask fast enough. "At home? How the fuck did he get Laura's personal number? Wait. How the hell did he know to even call her? Why call her? And why so late? Does he have a friend in the guards?"

"All good questions. I'm happy to answer them because this is where the story gets good."

"Oh, man." I prop my pillows up against the back of the pullout couch and yawn.

"Yes. He does have a buddy. Dude let him use his cellphone. Laura knew it was from the jail because she heard a hushed conversation right before Ryland said his goodbyes and hung up. Someone said rounds are about to start. He needs his phone back because if another guard catches them, they'll both be in trouble. It clinched it for her when she heard a door clanging open before Ryland hung up faster than a charging bull."

"What the fuck is going on with this asshole?"

"Somehow, he got info about the accident you were on yesterday with Jimothy. He called her on her personal cellphone. He said he got her number from one of his cop friends down here. Guess who?"

I narrow my eyes. "I'm kicking your ass if you say the guard."

"Guess we'll be wrestlin'. The guard. Who happens to be Laura's ex husband."

I chew the inside of my cheek as I let out a low growl. "Always wondered what happened to that asshole."

"Laura answered because it was his phone. They parted amicably. He's never called her at two in the morn' before," Mateo drawls. I can tell he's tired just by the way the Southern in his voice comes out far more than it usually does.

"So, he called Laura with her ex's phone from jail to do what? What did he want with Jimothy?"

"Not sure yet how he found out about Jimothy, but according to Preston, Laura told him he said something about how he was looking for Jimothy in connection to a case he's working out of Minnesota. He said he went to his house, but he wasn't there. He was asking her to help him locate him. He'd like an APB put out on him. If anyone finds him, haul him in. He's working on a warrant."

"He was already in custody when I was arriving at the accident scene. What the fuck is he trying to pull?"

"Laura found it pretty suspicious. 'Specially after you filled her in with everything going on, including Jimothy. She called Preston, then the Sheriff. He's supposed to be transported by the Marshalls back to

Minnesota tomorrow. Texas doesn't want anything to do with him, and his parole officer wants his ass back up there. Issued a warrant just yesterday when he missed his weekly check in."

"What… the… fuck… is happening?"

"I'm heading to Wako now to talk to him. I woke up Troy. His guys are on alert, but I don't know. I think you should have him closer to you. Maybe let him stay in your house or some shit."

"Maybe that's a good idea. This is getting more and more fucked up. I need to talk to Krissy to see if she even knows this kid. There has to be a connection."

"I'll let you know what I find."

"Thanks, Mateo."

"You got it."

We both hang up, and I sigh. My head swivels to the door when I hear movement and some sniffling. By the sounds of it, Krissy just had a nightmare and can't sleep anymore. It's been an ongoing problem for her the entire time I've been here.

I get up with a yawn and pull a pair of gray sweats on. I leave the shirt off as I pad to the door. When I open it, Krissy looks at me like she's just been caught doing something wrong.

I cross my arms over my chest as I lean against the doorframe and point to her bedroom. "Shower first," I rumble dominantly.

I know her routine well. She goes downstairs, lets Killer out, gets coffee, and paces while she drinks it. She reads the news on her phone and stares blankly at her TV. Then, she closes herself in her office. She doesn't eat. She doesn't come out of it for hours.

Not this time.

She keeps her eyes locked on me, but I can see how they roam my body. I feel the heat they leave behind, and I have to use all of my willpower, which is close to zero percent, to keep my dick down.

Finally, she nods and scurries to her bathroom. She closes the door quietly behind her. I don't move an inch until I hear her shower running. Only then do I reach down and grip my painfully hard cock. Killer is watching me, panting.

"Yeah, yeah. I'm sure it's happened to you, too."

He tilts his head and licks his chops. His pointed ears twitch as if he's really hearing and understanding what I'm saying.

"She thinks you're great. I think you're an asshole. You know that, right?"

He chuffs and turns. If I didn't know better, I'd swear he rolls his eyes.

"See? That's what I mean. What other dog does shit like that?" I push off the wall as he prances down the stairs. I follow him and let him outside. I turn on the kitchen light and start the coffee. No way either of us are getting through this without a load of this delectable nectar.

I set to making oatmeal. As the water is boiling, I start cutting up strawberries and bananas. I made it once, and Krissy practically gobbled it up. I also noticed she had far more energy that day. While I don't think she eats bad, I do think adding a few additional things to her diet might do her good.

By the time the oatmeal and toast are done, I hear Krissy making her way quietly down the stairs. When she reaches the kitchen, her head is down. I know her nightmare must've been a bad one. I need to tread carefully.

She sits down at the breakfast nook in front of a bowl I've set out for her. I set the toast down and kiss her head before letting Killer in. The gesture is sweet and simple. It's so comfortable and natural to me that it's almost scary, but also so easy that I feel like I've been doing it for years.

When I sit down across from her after feeding Killer, she's looking at me in wonder and awe, but her eyes are red and bloodshot.

I lay my hand on the table, palm up, inviting her to take it. After a few moments of staring at it, she does. "Baby, what happened? Talk to me."

She focuses on my thumb rubbing soothing circles over the top of her silky smooth hand. It takes her several moments to answer. I'm not sure she's going to until she takes a deep breath. "I have a recurring nightmare of the gang rape. There's always something a little bit different each time, but essentially, it's the same each night I have it. I have other nightmares of beatings and things I've endured, but that one…" She trails off. "It's the most repeated one. The one that gets me the most. I still don't know what I did to deserve it," she whispers.

I can't help but move to her. I kneel in front of her, not letting go of her hand, my heart fucking breaking for how shattered she is. I take her other one and kiss them both as I look at her. "Nothing about what happened is your fault, Krissy. Nothing. You didn't do anything to deserve anything that happened to you. I don't care how many times you need me to say that. I'll say it every single day for the rest of my days if that's what you need from me."

I watch the tears fill her eyes. She says nothing. She doesn't even look at me, but before I know what's happening, she's flinging herself into my arms. I steady us both before we topple to the ground and hug her as tightly as I can to my chest. She buries her face in my neck and shoulder as she cries. I stand with her in my arms and carry her to the chair I was sitting in. I hold her in my lap and let her cry as I run my fingers through her satin locks.

♡♡♡

Hours later, after Krissy cried herself out and we both ate our breakfast, I sit with her on her couch holding her close. I know I can't waste any more time.

I kiss the top of her head again. I've been doing it randomly all morning as she relaxes and comes back to herself.

"I love when you do that," she whispers. "It makes me feel like I'm yours." She's been gripping the waistband of my sweats since we sat down here. It's done a lot of things to my body that would make my mother ashamed, but all that matters is it brings her comfort. I'm glad to know kissing her on her head brings her joy.

"I'm glad. I don't intend to stop unless you tell me to. And you are mine."

She pauses as if she's processing my words. "And you'd respect me if I said no?" she asks after several moments of silence. I can hear the bravery it took her to say that in her voice.

"No means no. Anyone who doesn't respect that needs to be slathered with honey and left in the woods tied to a tree."

She looks up at me. "Why do I think you'd actually do that?"

I grin a little evilly. "I probably would."

She giggles. "I'd like to see it." She tucks her head back into my chest.

I take a deep breath. "Honey, I don't want to do this, especially after the night you had, but I do need to talk to you."

I feel the second she stiffens. Her grip on my sweats tighten, but I don't think she even realizes it. "Okay," she says nervously. She keeps her eyes down, focusing on my thighs.

I hug her a little tighter. "I'm not upset with you, baby. I just have a couple of questions I need some answers to. I have a feeling you were going to ask me how my day was yesterday before I moved too quickly and scared you. I don't ever want you to think you can't ask me about that. If I don't want to talk about it, I won't. But I'm never going to shut you down. I'm not going to hurt you. I won't yell at you or belittle you. And the answer to that question, beautiful, is the day wasn't too great. It started slow, but got progressively worse."

For the first time in hours, Krissy moves her hand. Instead of gripping my sweats, she moves to hug me. I love the feel of her arms around me. There's nothing better in the world. "I'm sorry your day wasn't good."

I rub my hand up and down her arm. "Do you know anyone named Jimothy Rivers?"

Krissy sucks in a breath and looks up at me with wide eyes. Fear and surprise meld together behind her irises. "How do you know about him?"

I barely hear her words because she's speaking so quietly, but her reactions has me curious. "Well, I've been dealing with him a couple years now. He's a good kid, but he's reckless. He's been in a lot of trouble. I've helped him out where I could, but yesterday was bad. He almost killed himself and four others. Two girls on their way to Austin to go shopping, and a father and son. Jimothy himself ended up trapped in his car upside down. The fire department had to cut him out."

"That's not possible." Krissy quickly stands and hugs herself as she shakes her head. "Not possible," she whispers to herself over and over again.

I furrow my brows but choose to watch her and continue. "When State Patrol got there, things took a pretty fucked up turn. Found out where Ryland is, though. State arrested him for his parole violation. He ain't supposed to be out of Minnesota without permission." She pauses with her hand on her heart and stares at me in shock. "He's being extradited today, but he was asking about Jimothy. Kinda strange considering we were dealing with him right then. Said he was your son."

She scoffs before sinking into a chair and rubbing her head. "Jimothy is dead. He died during childbirth. I never got to even meet him. I was so excited when my parents came to get me from my grandparents' house. That all changed when they said he didn't make it."

I furrow my brows, confused. "So, he'd be your brother."

"Would be. If he was alive. Which he's not. He died eighteen years ago." She curls into herself. "What the hell is happening right now?" she whispers to herself.

"I don't know. But you can bet your pretty ass I'm finding out." I pick up my phone and fill Mateo in on every detail I just learned. When I hang up, I fill Krissy in on everything that Mateo told me earlier.

When I'm finished, Krissy is pacing so restlessly that I know just what she needs. Without a word, I lead her upstairs and tell her to get dressed. We both do it quickly. I make a couple of sandwiches and grab some drinks for us. I grab some treats for Killer and extra water.

"What are we doing?" Krissy asks me softly.

"I know you don't like straying too far from the sanctity of your home, baby, but I have somewhere secluded I want to show you. You're restless. You need peace, and this is the best place in the area that can give you that. It's not far, and you'll be with me, so you'll be safe."

"I -"

"Krissy. You need this." I don't hesitate to tug her close to me so I can hug her. I lean down and kiss her neck. "Please trust me," I rumble against her sensitive skin.

She breathes steadily with me as I sway gently with her. Slowly, she starts to relax, little by little, but I'll take what I can get. Finally, she takes a deep breath. "I trust you," she whispers into my chest.

The words are simple. Sweet.

But to me, they feel like balloons are simultaneously being blown up inside me and let go. My heart expands. My stomach follows. I feel like I'm floating.

She trusts me.

Trust.

It's a hard word for her. Difficult for her to do.

But she does with me. She trusts me. I can feel it radiating off her and sinking into me.

Fucking trusts.

I'll never break that. Never shatter it under any circumstances. I want her to trust me. Feel safe with me.

I need her to.

Chapter Nine

♡ Krissy ♡

(Three Months Later)

I snuggle into Caden and hug his arms around me. My back pushes into his chest as I blink my eyes open. It's still dark, and I yawn, unsure of what woke me up. It's only five in the morning. For the middle of Fall, it still feels so stiflingly warm, even with the air on in my house.

Caden tightens his arms around me and buries his face in my hair. We've never done anything more than cuddle and kiss. He started sleeping in my bed with me nightly because I kept having night terrors that got increasingly worse and worse. Not even Killer could keep them away. I don't have them when Caden's holding me. He keeps everything bad away.

My thoughts.

My PTSD.

My spirals into dark and deep depression.

Caden makes me happy. Calm. Collected. He makes me feel like a normal, rational being. Someone who isn't crazy with insane thoughts and paranoia that someone is going to jump out from around the corner and drag me into the unknown.

But he'll never know any of that. I won't tell him because I'm afraid it will make him run. I'm falling in love with him, but I don't want him to know that. I feel like it would push him away, and that's the last thing I want. If things could stay the way they are right now forever, I'd be content with that.

I decide to get up and see if I can turn the air up a little bit to cool it off. It must've been warmer than I thought it was outside last night because it feels like it's getting even warmer in here than it was when I first woke up just a few minutes ago.

Caden tightens his grip even more and pulls me closer to him. Close enough that I can feel every ridge of his body. Every hard muscle.

Especially the one poking against my backside.

My eyes widen, and I try to wiggle free.

"Mmm...," Caden growls raspily. "Stop moving." His voice is heavy with sleep.

I squeak quietly when I feel his erection get even harder. "I think... you might want me to get up." I can feel his smile against the back of my neck, and it makes me blush several unnamed colors of red. "Caden, you're -"

"Hard? I know. That tends to happen when a man wakes up next to a beautiful woman." He pauses. "Or man. Depends on his preference."

"But -"

"Shh... it's normal, baby. Give him a few minutes. He'll go down."

I bite my lip, my face darkening even more.

Caden pops his head up. "Unless you're uncomfortable." He starts to pull away, and I quickly realize that he's suddenly scared that I'm not consenting to what's happening. Consent is a huge thing with him. Especially after what happened to me.

I grip his arm and tug him back to me. "I don't want to get up yet," I whisper. "I was just surprised. I've never woken up like that before with you."

I feel him smile against my neck before he kisses it. "Because I usually move before you feel it."

I bite my lip and blush. After a few moments, I finally manage to speak what I'm thinking. "Maybe you shouldn't..."

Caden kisses my shoulder. "Then I won't." He kisses up my neck, to my jaw, to my lips. One of his strong hands cups my cheek and turns my face to his so he can kiss me deeper.

I shiver and sink into him. When his tongue meets mine, I lose all control. I turn in his arms and push him on his back before climbing on top of him, straddling him. Without waiting for him to do anything, like reject me, I lean down and kiss him hard. I'm trembling. I don't know what's gotten into me, but all I want is for him to devour me with his mouth. Possess me completely. Show me I'm his and he's not going anywhere.

As if he's reading my mind, Caden slides one hand to my ass and the other up my back. He tangles his fingers in my hair and grips the back of my neck. Taking complete control away from me, he pushes me down onto his hard cock and angles my head so he can plunge his tongue into my mouth and claim me like I need him to.

I gasp into his mouth and whimper when he pushes his dick against me. The trembling becomes more and more intense and uncontrollable. I push my fingers into his hair and tug as my tongue dances with his. He rubs his dick against my center until I can't stop myself from exploding. I scream into his mouth, but he holds me tight and close. I jerk against him while I ride my orgasm. Caden's kiss only deepens as he holds me while I come.

"I got you, baby," he rumbles against my lips. "You're okay. I got you."

I pant for several minutes as I come back to myself with my face buried in the crook of his neck. Slowly, the trembling subsides and embarrassment takes over. When I finally realize the totality of what I did, I suddenly can't breathe.

"Oh my God." I try to get up quickly, but Caden only tightens his grip.

"Shh... you didn't do anything wrong, and I'm not letting you run after I just witnessed something so beautiful. I'm not allowing you to be embarrassed about taking what you need from me in the moment. Now, be my good girl and relax. That was fucking intense, and you need this. You need to feel that I'm not going anywhere, and I'm not going to ever condemn you or make you feel like shit for having an orgasm or for anything else."

Caden has no idea how quickly his words calm me. How my erratic heartbeat immediately calms the second his arms tighten around me. As he holds me tight with one arm, he allows his other hand to soothingly move up and down my back.

After another few moments pass, I take a deep, calming breath. "Tell me about the retirement party again."

Caden chuckles and kisses me just below my ear. He knows how much I love hearing about it. I love the things that happened that involve him because it helps me to see that he's really just an average person. He's the same man in the uniform as he is without it. And the man out of the uniform is the one I'm so very much in love with. Even if it can only be in my mind.

Caden's fingers run gently through my hair and tug the ends. The repetitive motion does so much more to calm my racing mind. "Lieutenant Bill Camden. The guy's my hero. I became the cop I am today because of him. When I went into it, it was because I wanted to help people, but I had an attitude. I still have it, but it's different. I learned how to command authority without words because of him. I learned everything I know today because of him and my own experiences, but one of the biggest things I learned was compassion. Not everyone needs a ticket. Not everyone needs a night in jail. Sometimes, people just need a break or a hug. I wanted him to stick around for my whole career, but I knew that wouldn't happen in real life. Stress from the job takes a toll on a cop. That's why our retirement eligibility is after twenty-five years, if we want our full pension, instead of a set age of sixty-seven. We could retire after twenty if we were okay with taking half. Or we can get our full pension if we are forced into retirement from some kind of medical issue. PTSD can be included in that."

He kisses my temple, and I melt into him. He massages the back of my neck before going back to rub his hand up and down my back. Even more than his voice; his words, it's the strong hands and safety I feel in his arms that's really it for me.

"It was my honor telling stories about him and giving him his retirement plaque. Retiring his badge number. But my favorite part was seeing his joy at reliving those memories." He kisses my head. "I'm glad he's able to be out there enjoying life."

I smile into his neck. "I love hearing about your relationship with him, but I think I love when you tell that story best of all. It really shows how amazing you are."

A low rumble vibrates through his chest. "He's one of the good ones. He sure liked you."

I blush. "I liked him, too. His party after was fun. It really seemed like he was a staple of the community. So many people showed up."

"He had a great career. The relationships he built over his career is something I aspire to."

I smile again. "Personally, I think you've reached it. I know I haven't really been out all that much, but the things we have done together, it seems everyone knows and respects you."

"Speaking of going places. I'm proud of you for the progress you've made with that. Have you thought more about the Halloween party at Walker Ranch?"

"Mmhmm. I really want to go. I love Halloween so much."

"Yeah?" Caden turns his face towards me and hugs me. "I have the perfect costumes."

"Ooh…" I shift and prop myself up. "What are they?"

He grins and kisses my chin. "The Pumpkin King and Sally."

My eyes widen. "Oh my God, really?" I squeak and kiss him. "*Nightmare Before Christmas* is one of my favorite movies of all time!"

Caden laughs and kisses me back. "I know. I was hoping you'd say yes. I already bought the costumes."

I sit up, still straddling him. "Yes! I'm so excited! I want to wear it now!"

He laughs again and runs his hands up my bare legs to my short sleep shorts. They stop on my butt. "They should be delivered to my house today. I got Jimothy a Lock costume. That's his favorite character from that movie." He swats my ass causing me to jerk and gasp at how hard he is. "Now, up. Or I'm going to make a mess of you."

I bite my lip. He looks at me like he wants to devour me, and I almost let him. He reaches up and tugs my lip loose before sitting up and taking my mouth with his once more. He kisses me until I see stars. When he pulls back, I'm not sure I even know my own name.

"You don't know how much I needed everything you just did," I whisper, though I have no idea how the words came out.

He smiles and hugs me. "I know you don't think I knew, but I did." He kisses my neck. "Now. Go take a shower. Jimothy is supposed to be coming over for breakfast."

"But it's still so early," I whine teasingly. Killer barks, and I roll my eyes when I look at him as Caden laughs. "You're a diva."

He bares his teeth before licking me. I laugh and snuggle him. I kiss his nose and pull away as he jumps off the bed and prances to the door.

"That means he needs to relieve himself and wants food," Caden says matter-of-factly.

I giggle. "Since when do you speak dog?"

"Since last week when he finally decided I'm worthy enough to have my own spot on your bed without trying to fucking steal it." He smirks.

I laugh again. "Newsflash, Lieutenant Gorgeous. That dog has adored you since he first laid eyes on you."

His smirk grows into a cocky grin as he kisses my nose. "That might be true. Pretty sure I wouldn't be here if he hadn't decided I'm safe enough to be around his princess."

I tilt my chin in the air arrogantly, but teasingly. "Queen, obviously."

"My queen," he says so possessively, I nearly come all over again. "His princess."

"Yes, daddy," I giggle as I jump out of bed and sprint to the bathroom.

"Fuck me. Keep calling me that, and you'll end up against the wall while I fuck you!" he yells loud enough for me to hear behind the door that I've slammed shut.

I giggle again. "Anything you say…, daddy!" I can feel my cheeks redden when he groans, and I can't stop the next giggle when it bubbles out of me.

"I'll be in the bathroom downstairs painting the shower!"

I crack up at the thought of him unable to hold back and coming all over my shower walls.

"And when I'm done, you can lick me clean!"

I let out a loud squeak. "Caden!"

"You started it, baby girl! Now, hurry up! I want a few minutes alone with you before I need to start cooking!"

The promise of his words has me hurrying to undress and step in the shower. A few minutes alone with him means more kisses and hugging, and I'm really starting to love that, even though I want so much more with him.

To ease my raging hormones, I let my thoughts wander to Jimothy. My little brother that I thought was dead. It's only been a few months, but I feel like we've known each other forever. It's like no time was lost. We clicked with each other, and that was it. He's already very protective of his big sis, but what I love the most is that I can see there's been such a change in him. He's so much happier than he was when we first met.

Honestly, so am I. I feel like a piece of me that I've always known was missing, but never paid attention to, is filled.

And with Caden by my side, no matter which way I get him, I feel whole for the first time in my life.

Chapter Ten

♡ Caden ♡

(Halloween)

"So, what you're saying is we keep this from her and let her enjoy her fucking life, right?" I growl low to my big brother, Troy. He's two years older than me and a couple of inches taller, but I've always been the one who stood up to him the most when he got bossy growing up.

Troy narrows his eyes. "You want her out here not knowing that fucking prick ex of hers is out of jail again?" he drawls as he crosses his arms over his chest.

I glance over my shoulder. Krissy is enjoying dancing with Jimothy. The smile plastered on her face is starting to come out more and more, and I refuse to take that from her.

I turn back to Troy. "Listen. Don't ruin this for her. You have tabs on him, right? He's got an ankle bracelet. He's tethered to his fucking house, right?"

Troy shakes his head but keeps his voice low enough for just me to hear. "You know as well as I do that people can slip out of those. He's an ex cop. We can't discount that and underestimate him. Guard up at all times. You know that."

"Then give her tonight, man. Please. She's happy. Enjoying herself. I'll tell her after the party."

"I also want her at your house. Your security is better."

I rub my head. "Fuck." I know she hates the very idea of leaving her house. That's her safe place. If she can't feel safe there, how is she supposed to feel safe anywhere? That's why I haven't already asked her to move in with me until this shit with Ryland is finished. I can't bring myself to take away the little bit of security she feels.

"I know, Caden. Trust me," Troy says, his voice softening. "I know she feels safe where she is, but she's not. There are too many places I can't protect or cover with cameras. If we can at least get her to agree to stay with you for the time being, I can get some guys to clear some trees and other shit, so I can cover her property."

"That's a conversation you need to have with her, Troy." I look over my shoulder again when I hear her laugh. It makes me smile. "We done?" I ask him when I turn towards him.

He sighs. "Fine. But she's gonna notice the extra security, so don't hold off too fucking long."

I give him a quick nod and reach Krissy just as she throws her head back to laugh at something Jimothy said. It's the most adorable thing I've ever heard, but also one of the sexiest. She doesn't even have to try, and she has my dick hard as granite for her.

I slide an arm around her waist and possessively pull her to my side. Not because of Jimothy. I don't have a problem with her brother. I'm not fucking psycho. It's because I can see so many looking at her. Some are still curious about her, so they observe her. But others look at her hungrily. My act of possession is for them. I'm telling them she'll never be theirs.

She's fucking mine.

"Hi," she says with a smile I'm sure she reserves just for me. Her entire face lights up. Her eyes sparkle.

Like always happens, my grin matches hers as I look down at her. "Hey, pretty girl. What I miss?"

She giggles. "Jimothy was telling me about the first time you pulled him over and called the people who adopted him."

I laugh as I look at Jimothy. "You fucking knew I wasn't going to reach them."

He shrugs with a grin. "They love those cruises."

"I ended up escorting him home, and he roped me into buying him a damn pizza." I look down at Krissy. "And then made me eat it with him. Worst night of my life."

Jimothy cracks up. "The greatest part was that he actually ended up playing video games with me, too. I made him a pro at Halo."

Krissy giggles. "He said you kept dying, but it only made you more determined."

"Only after he threw my controller," Jimothy chips in, a tease in the undertone of his voice.

I smile again. "Yeah. Onto his beanbag chair so it didn't get hurt."

"Sounds like you guys have built a good relationship."

Jimothy smiles softly. "Yeah, he's been the only one I could count on, but also the only one who gave enough of a shit to really be the disciplinarian I needed. I was doing really fucking good, too. Until I found out those assholes ruined college for me."

"They didn't ruin everything for you, buddy," I rumble. "We got you in community college this year. That, at least, gets you a headstart on your four years. Get those generals out of the way."

He gives me a sheepish smile before heading for a fruit punch at the drink bar. I turn to Krissy and wrap her in my arms. She instantly relaxes into me, and I love that I can make her feel safe enough to let go like this; to let all of the tension leave her body as she breathes out a long, slow breath.

I kiss the top of her head and sway gently with her to the music that only I hear in my head; the music only she makes me hear. "Doing okay, baby?"

"Mmhmm. But I think I'm ready to call it quits for the night."

I fight every cell in my body not to lift her in my arms and carry her to my truck while kissing her until she blacks out. Instead, I satiate myself by taking her hand. This past week has been hell. We've spent a lot of time making out like two teenagers, but I always manage to pull myself away before things go too far. I don't want to do anything with her if she's not ready. I don't want either one of us leading with our hormones and not our brains.

Every time I pull away, I can see the hurt in her eyes. I try to kiss it away, but I can tell she's losing what little confidence I've helped her build. It's time to have that conversation with her.

I just don't fucking like that we now have this other shit hanging over us. As I lead her to my truck after grabbing Jimothy, I squeeze her hand. I tell myself it's for her and her comfort, but it's not. It's for me. It's to keep me grounded because I know that I can't talk to her about anything else between us until I tell both her and Jimothy about Ryland being out of jail and on house arrest.

Troy is right. It doesn't really matter if Ryland is saddled with an ankle monitor or not. He's an ex cop. I'm sure he knows how to get out of it. Lots of people out there know the tricks. Not that difficult to learn.

When we pull into my driveway, Nate, Jimothy's bodyguard, is waiting outside, and it causes me to raise an eyebrow. I glance at my phone in the cupholder of my truck and see a missed call from Troy.

"Shit," I rumble under my breath low enough so no one can hear. I stop my truck and Nate starts walking towards me just as Jimothy opens his door. "Stay in the truck for a second, man," I say as I quickly get out and jump to the ground. I close the door and meet Nate halfway between my house and truck. "What's going on?"

"Ryland bought a plane ticket. Ash caught it," he says to me, glancing at my truck. Ash is Troy's tech guy and hacker. I don't pretend to know how the fuck he does what he does. "He's heading to Dallas."

"Can't you guys do something about that?"

"Already have. Troy knows you won't like it, but he wants us to allow it. Let him come. See what he does."

"Yeah, don't like it."

"Look, man. I know you run by different rules, but we're good at what we do. No one is getting to her or Jimothy."

"You better fucking make sure of that. When's the flight?"

"Christmas. The week before. Return flight is right before Christmas."

"So, less than a week? Why? What's the play?"

"That's what we want to know, man. We think he's looking for info on her, but we don't know why Dallas."

I run my fingers through my hair and groan. "This needs to fucking end."

"We're playing the long game, Caden. You know Troy knows what he's doing. When he goes down, we want him to go down for life. And you know he'll keep you posted. I met you out here because Troy doesn't want you guys at her house tonight. I already grabbed Killer and some clothes for you both. He thinks Ryland has an accomplice and wants to figure out who. Your house is -"

"More secure. Yeah. He's fucking forcing my hand, here, and he fucking knows it." I turn and head for the passenger side of my truck. I open Krissy's door and hold out a hand while looking in the backseat at Jimothy as Krissy takes my hand. "Straight inside. Clean up. Meet me in the living room. Go."

Jimothy does exactly what I say. I turn to Krissy and wrap my other arm around her waist. I lift her down as she watches me fearfully. I hate that her mood instantly dropped. I hate that she's afraid. I squeeze her hand as I close the door and lead her inside.

"What's happening, Caden?"

"Not out here, baby girl. We need to get inside."

She snaps her mouth shut and keeps up with my steps, molding her entire body to my arm. I don't need to see her eyes to know they are darting all over the place, and I hate that I can't just tell her out here. I might not agree with him all of the time, but when it comes to people's safety, Troy is the best. He didn't reach the level of success that he did by not being good at what he does.

Just before we reach the door, I hear a car pulling into my driveway. I glance over my shoulder while pushing Krissy in front of me so I can shield her from any threats with my body. The car stops next to my truck and cuts the lights. I realize it's Troy and let out a breath of relief.

The second we're inside, Nate locks the door and heads for the living room behind Troy. I lead Krissy to my bedroom in silence, but I know she's scared. I can feel it. I close the door once we're in my room and pull her in front of me so I can wrap her in my arms. I know she needs to feel comfort and safety above all else right now.

"I know you're scared, baby. I'm sorry. I got some information tonight, and then Nate gave me more. I'll explain everything downstairs, but first, let's get out of these costumes, okay?"

She sniffles as her small hands grip the fabric of my outfit. "It's Ryland... He's back."

My grip tightens. I walk her to the bed without letting her go. "He's not here. He's in Minnesota. But he's out. He's got an ankle monitor." I sit down and pull her into my lap, keeping her protected in my embrace. "He bought a ticket to go to Dallas. The week before Christmas. He's going back before Christmas. It makes me think that he's going through the proper channels to get a traveler's permit through his parole officer."

"But…," she murmurs into my chest, "he can't travel with a monitor…"

I take a deep breath. This is the second hardest part of this conversation. "He's only on the monitor for thirty days. He's playing it smart. He's not asking for a permit down here right away. He's trying to prove himself."

She nods into my shoulder. To her credit, she doesn't cry. She's not even stiff in my arms. She just hugs me and lets me hold her while swaying gently.

But I know her. I know she's deep in thought. I know I'm going to have a fight on my hands keeping her from shutting down again. I've come so far with her. I'm not letting her go back because of that asshole.

She needs to know she's safe now. Nothing is going to hurt her. Not with me around.

She's mine.

All mine.

And I'm going to prove it to her.

Chapter Eleven

♡ Krissy ♡

(Christmas Day)

My life since Halloween has been a literal real life fairytale. I fall more and more in love with Caden each day. And he continuously shows that I'm not too much for him. That he's sticking around, no matter what happens. No matter how slowly I want to take things, or how afraid I am to take the next step with him, even though I want that so badly.

He's proving that not all cops are bad cops. Not all cops hide behind their badge and expect other cops to stick up for them and defend them when they do awful things. Ryland and his friends are just a few rotten apples in a sea of so many good and shiny red ones.

It's also changed drastically. I've been living with Caden. Jimothy has been with us. I feel like everything is perfect. I've never been more content. I feel at home here, but I've discovered that it's not the place. I could be anywhere, and as long as I have Caden. Caden is where my home is.

Which is why I've decided that tonight is the night. I've been given the okay to move back to my house, but I don't want to. I want to stay here with Caden. So, tonight has to be the night. It has to be the right time.

"You look so lost in thought," Caden rumbles against my neck right before his slightly rough lips kiss it. I shiver and lean back against him when his arms lock around me.

I'm staring out the window at the lake. I've seen snow, plenty of it, but there's something so magical about the way it's falling so lightly here in Piper Falls. The weather seems to be having a complete meltdown. We had the hottest summer on record, but our winter seems to be coldest. Piper Falls hasn't seen snow in many years. Yet, here we are, snow falling gently from the sky. It creates the illusion of a winter wonderland. Not much snow, just enough to blanket the ground in white and coat the trees.

"Just thinking...," I say wistfully.

Caden starts swaying gently with me. I tilt my head just enough so his cheek is pressed against mine. He has to bend, but he doesn't seem to mind. He seems to be just as at peace as I am. "What are you thinking about, baby?"

We're in his living room, and I keep expecting Jimothy to walk in and make a comment about Caden's arms around me. He loves teasing us when he catches us in any kind of intimate position. Caden kissed me while I was making dinner yesterday, and Jimothy made a gagging noise before he cracked up laughing and grabbed a water. The three of us get along so well. I've loved this feeling. The feeling of belonging somewhere.

"Just... how great things have been." I can't word it any differently. Everything with him has been incredible. Caden has shown me an entirely new world. One where I'm treated with the utmost respect. One where I'm cherished in all of the ways I should be and supported in everything I do.

"They have been great, haven't they?"

I smile softly, potentially having to leave if this doesn't go well hanging heavy on my heart. "The best I've ever had. I don't want it to...," I pause and take a deep breath, "end."

He rumbles out a chuckle as he smiles and hugs me closer. "Who said anything has to end?"

I wrap my arms around his and entwine my fingers with his. "It's just that my house is ready, so I'll have to go back to it."

"Have to?" He squeezes my fingers and kisses the corner of my mouth. "I don't think anyone here said you had to do anything."

My heart stops and picks up pace at the same time. How that's possible, I don't know, but I feel like I'm a jet plane ready to take off. "I just thought... that... was the plan," I whisper nervously. I hope with everything I am that he says I can stay. With him.

Forever...

"The plan is what you want it to be, baby." He kisses down my cheek to my neck. He trails the hand I'm not holding up my arm. His fingertips leave goosebumps, and I melt into him.

My eyes fall closed, and I let him do what only he can. Quiet my mind and calm every nervous fiber of my being. I let out a quiet breath. "I don't want to leave," I say quietly. Words I've only ever said to myself. Never out loud.

My heart knows what he's going to say. But my mind... it goes crazy with thoughts that I can't stop. It says he's going to throw me out. That he doesn't really want me. That I'm not good enough for him. I'll never be good enough for him or anyone. I'm not what he wants. Don't fall in love.

"Then don't. I love having you here."

His words hit my core like an electric shock, and I can't help but squeeze my thighs together, feeling ridiculous that he has that effect on me. It takes longer to sink into the rest of me, but as they do, I start to feel warmer and warmer. More relaxed. Confident in what we're building.

I lean my head back against his shoulder and bare my neck to him. He can't seem to resist kissing it, growling against it, or nipping it before he sucks on it. My favorite thing is when he marks me. I love it because it makes me feel like his, even though I know I am. Sometimes, I just don't listen to myself. Seeing that mark on my neck, or anywhere else he chooses to leave it, is the reminder I need when I'm in my own mind.

"Then... I won't..." I bite my lip and look up at him.

He growls low in his throat. "Fuck, you know I love when you do that." His hand slowly caresses its way down my body until it reaches the waistband of my jeans. He kisses me slowly before putting more pressure on my lips.

He hooks his thumb near the button of my jeans, and I'd give anything if he slid his hand lower. I know he's waiting on me for that.

We've had extensive talks about how he'll only do what I ask of him. Only what I'm ready for. I'm ready for so much, but I don't know how to tell him.

His fingers graze the outside of my breasts while he kisses along my shoulders and back to the other side of my neck. He growls low against my sensitive flesh. I feel the vibration of his voice moving up his chest that's flush against my back.

Once again, I let my head fall back against his shoulder. His thumb rubs slow, smooth circles on the underside of my right boob, but it's the hand that's lower that brings the moan out. His fingertips dance near my zipper and each soft touch feels like my core has been zapped with electricity.

"I love that you're so responsive to me, sweet girl." He nips my jawline before making his way up to my lips once more. "I bet you taste as sweet as the finest maple."

I can't say anything. My body has taken control now. "Mmm...," I moan as I grip his wrist. My hand trembles slightly, but I need to feel him more than I need to breathe. He's my air now.

I push his hand down inch by inch. The closer he gets to where I need him; crave him, the wetter I get for him. I can feel my panties getting more and more damp by the second.

Right before I get his hand where I need it to be, he stops me. I whimper, but he covers my mouth with his. "I need words, baby. Do you want me to touch you here?"

I nod. "Yes," I whisper. *Oh God, yes.*

He moves his hand the rest of the way. My hand still grips his wrist when he cups my pussy and starts rubbing his palm against my clit while squeezing with just enough pressure to make me both gasp and moan at the same time.

He rubs in a circle and slowly until I'm so worked up, I can hardly focus. I don't need to see his reflection in the window to know he's smirking.

He inches his other hand up my tit, and I arch into him. "Words, Krissy," he growls in my ear commandingly enough to make my knees weak.

"Please," I beg breathily.

With no further words, his hand is cupping both of my tits. He squeezes them both in turn while letting his thumb circle my nipples until they're both pebbled. My vision seems to blur with pleasure, but it's not enough.

I can't feel him enough.

"More...," I rasp into his kiss as he swallows my moans.

Caden grins and nips my lip. He drops his hand to my waist while still gripping my pussy as he rubs and squeezes. I move against his hand, craving more friction. He slides his other hand underneath my off-white cashmere sweater. His fingertips leave scorch marks along my skin as he brushes his hand up and traces my nipples over my bra before he goes back to fondling them both.

"Tell me what you want," he growls in my ear.

"You."

"You have me." He slaps my pussy, causing me to gasp and jump as I writhe into his hand.

"Caden!"

"Shh... Don't want to wake up Jimothy, do we?" He pinches my nipples and flicks the other one. I puff out a soft sigh as I shake my head. "Good girl. Do you want my fingers inside you?"

My whole body ignites and hums as my pussy drips for him. My panties are soaked. "Yes," I hiss as I turn my head towards his face. I capture his mouth with mine.

While his tongue dominantes mine, he swiftly undoes my jeans with one hand, not letting my tits go for a second as he lavishes them with attention. I'm already so close. I know the second I feel him, he'll have me gushing for him in seconds. I've never been this wet for anyone in my life. I've never craved someone the way I do him.

I try to lean forward to brace myself against the window, but Caden holds me tight against his body as he slides his calloused hand into my panties. He circles my clit with his thumb and sucks my lower lip into his mouth before sliding one long finger as deeply inside me as it can go.

"Don't scream," he whispers, but I can hear the dominance in his deep voice as he looks deep into my eyes.

My nails dig into his arms as I ride his finger. "Yes, sir." I keep my voice low, but I don't want to be quiet. I want to scream his name.

"Sir? What happened to 'daddy'?" He grins teasingly, but his eyes are dark enough to be mistaken for coal. There's a dangerous glimmer that makes me want to do everything he tells me to, not asks. I want him to be in complete control, and that's not something I've wanted from anyone else.

It's new. Different. But it feels so right, that not giving in would make me feel like the biggest sinner. If being a sinner gets me this, though, I'll be the greatest one anyone has ever seen. I thought me calling him daddy was just a way to tease him, but now I realize just how much it turns him on. I can feel him against my back.

"Whatever daddy wants," I finally manage to squeak out over the pleasure he's building. When he smiles and he lights up the entire room, heat rises to my cheeks.

"Good girl," he rumbles, pulling me against him tighter as he enters a second finger like he thinks I need to be rewarded for good behavior. Just his words having me soaking his finger, but when he enters a second one, I clench.

"Oh God, yes!" I whisper-scream as my pussy pulses around his fingers. My thighs start trembling as he thrusts hard, deep, and fast while he crooks his fingers against a spot inside me.

I try to cover my mouth, knowing I'm about to break his rule and scream, but I've never felt anything like what he's making me feel like right at this second. My entire body quakes for him. My heart is beating fast. My stomach is tight, but it tightens even more. Tingles erupt like a firework, and I know I'm close.

Caden thrusts faster until I feel like I'm losing my mind. I know he knows I'm getting closer to breaking his rule and shouting, but like a dark angel, he slaps a hand over my mouth just before he makes me forget my name.

My eyes roll back in my head. "Caden!" I scream behind his hand. He doesn't stop thrusting when my pussy starts clenching uncontrollably around him. I can feel myself soaking his fingers as the waves of my orgasm rushes over me.

His thrusts slow as my climax starts to calm. The thumb that was furiously rubbing my clit with the perfect amount of pressure gently releases. His other arm moves down and hooks under my breasts. He holds me up while he slowly slides his hand out of my panties. I feel like jello;

my limbs heavy. If he weren't holding me so tightly, I'd surely be on the ground.

My eyes snap open wide when I hear a door open. I quickly button and zip my jeans again as Caden chuckles. "Next time you come without my permission or scream my name instead of 'daddy', I'm spanking your ass a pretty shade of red." His words come out a low growl against my neck. I'm still trembling from the pleasure, but his words set me off all over again.

"Mmm…" I can't formulate words, so I nod, trying to show I'm agreeing. He helps me to the breakfast bar and helps me sit on a stool. I'm grateful because I'm close to simply melting into a puddle.

"Shit. Left my phone upstairs." Caden kisses my neck as I hum another agreement. "Morning, J. How'd you sleep?"

"Well enough to not want to get up. Stayed up late. Hoped I'd see Santa."

Caden laughs richly. "Well, he showed up sometime. Looks like there's presents under the tree."

Jimothy glances over his shoulder with a grin as he pours himself a cup of coffee and grins at Caden as Caden leaves the kitchen. I hear him jogging up the stairs as Jimothy leans on the counter across from me.

I eye him warily and raise a brow. "What did you hear?"

He grins. "Enough. Was it everything you dreamed?"

He's the only one I've opened up to, but I didn't say too much. Just that I wanted to stay with him and take things to the next level. "It was so much more. Oh my God." I put my head down. "Holy Christ. Change the subject." I look up at him.

"Okay, okay. That girl I met in my English class? She texted me last night. We talked for a while."

"Oh my God! That's so amazing! How long did you talk?"

Jimothy reaches into the fridge and grabs me a bottle of water. I take it and drink greedily, suddenly very thirsty. "It went good. So good that by the end we weren't just talking."

I giggle and set my bottle down. "That well, huh?"

"Yeah. Especially when we got to the video stuff."

"No more details." I laugh.

Jimothy grins. "For real, though. How badly did you want that to continue?"

I groan. "Well, let's just say that if I had my choice, I'd be bending over this counter right now. Or on it. Or against a wall. Not p-"

Jimothy clears his throat, interrupting me. I know the second I feel the chills start that Caden is right behind me. I'm way too shy to look. I know I've turned into a tomato.

"Jimothy," Caden says low, almost like a growl. "You might want to open up that gift leaning against the edge of the stone near the fireplace. And put some headphones on to cancel out the noise."

I sputter-squeak. Jimothy laughs and winks. I have no chance to say another word because Caden's hands suddenly grip my hips. He lifts me off the chair and tosses me possessively over his shoulder. He slaps my ass hard right before he bites it, then grips it. Hard.

"Oh my God," I breathe out, knowing I'm in for the ride of my life.

Chapter Twelve

♡ Caden ♡

Hearing her tell Jimothy where she could see herself with me was all I needed to break the very thin line that was holding my resolve together. I need her. I want nothing more than to taste her and feel my dick deep down her throat. And then I would love to pound into her until she sees colors. By the time I'm done with her, she's not going to be able to walk. Licking her essence off my fingers on the way up to grab my phone was enough to make me want to go feral on her.

I close the door behind me and toss her on the bed. She bounces and giggles as I tear off my sweater and toss it. She watches me with both curiosity and lust.

It's the lust that pushes me over the edge. I'm barely keeping control. I want to fucking ravish her, but I know better. She's not ready for how hard I want to take her. Holding back is making me sweat.

I stalk towards the bed after removing my jeans and boxer briefs. Her eyes widen as she watches me. She licks her lips, and I pounce. I cover her mouth with mine and kiss her with all I'm worth until we're both panting. She's pinned beneath me, but the way she's rubbing against me convinces me that she's ready. Her jeans are already wet from when I made her come just minutes ago, and I'm sure even more from how turned on she is now.

"I need your mouth on my dick right now, baby." I nip her lip before getting up. I'm straddling her, so I take her arms and pull her up with me. "First, clothes off. I need to see all of you."

I pull her shirt over her head before making quick work of her bra while she fumbles with the button on her jeans. Her eyes are on my dick, and that only makes me harder. Precome is already beading from my tip. She reaches for my length, I have greater plans. Her eyes snap to mine as I kiss her palm.

"Not yet, baby. If you touch me, I'm gonna embarrass myself." I gently push her down as she smiles brightly.

I grin and tug her jeans and underwear off her, exposing her beautiful, naked body to my hungry eyes. She lets her eyes wander all over my muscles and ridges just as I take in every curve, mound, a perfect line of her body. When I reach her pussy, I can see she's already glistening for me. Wet enough that I'm sure I'll have her dripping the second my tongue touches her.

I lay next to her on my back and reach down, stroking my length. She pushes up to her elbows and watches every movement. I don't miss her tongue when she licks the corner of her mouth where I'm sure a little drool just escaped from.

"I want you straddling my face. I need to taste you. And I need your mouth on my dick sucking me off."

She sits up the rest of the way and looks at me for direction. I guide her to the position I want her, her pussy above my mouth, and my long, thick cock just waiting to be devoured.

"What do I do?" she asks nervously.

I wrap my arms around her waist and lock them around her. "Suck."

Unable to hold back, I pull her down so she has no choice but spread her legs and smother me with her smooth, shaved, and incredibly sweet pussy. She's the perfect combination of salt and honey, and I don't waste a second. I start licking her; eating her pussy like a sugar cookie. I open my mouth wide and growl as my tongue darts inside her wetness.

She screams around my dick and tries to shift her weight up, but I don't let her. I keep my pace, licking her like she's the one thing I need to survive. Her small hand finally makes its way to my cock and I moan into her pussy when she starts stroking all of the places she can't reach with her mouth. Her tongue meets mine lash for lash. She strokes, rotating her wrist, and sucks with as much ferocity as I'm tasting her.

Her moans against my dick send vibrations right through me. I know I'm not going to last long. I can already feel a lighting bolt crashing down my spine. I'm harder than I've ever been in my life. Her spit mixing with my own precome is enough to make me lose it, but it's the hand making sure no part of my length is forgotten that really gets me. No one has ever given me the kind of pleasure she is right now.

Her thighs are trembling for me. Her pussy is quivering as she drips for me. "Fuck, Krissy. Come for me. Give me all of you, baby," I rumble into her pussy. I lick and suck her, flicking her clit with my tongue. I shake my head so my tongue hits her at angles she's not expecting.

I feel the second her pussy gives and clenches over my tongue. Her body quakes, and she screams around my dick.

It's damn near my undoing. While I let her ride my tongue through her orgasm, I grip her hair and tug so she comes off my dick. I want to come. Just not in her mouth. I have a much better idea.

I lick her clean because I'm not wasting a single drop of her. As soon as I have my fill of her, I let go of her hair and kiss her pussy before helping her off me. She looks disappointed that I'm not continuing when I sit up. I raise an eyebrow.

"I'm safe. And I'm on birth control. I -"

I grin and lean in. I kiss her to silence her and pull back slowly. "So am I. And I got a vasectomy years ago. I want to come inside of you, baby. Not in your mouth. Will you let me?"

She blushes shyly and nods as she looks down, clasping her hands between her thighs. I cup her cheek, and just as I open my mouth to tell her I need words, she speaks, "Yes, sir," she whispers.

I bite my lip to keep from grinning, but those aren't the words I want her to speak. "Care to correct that?"

Just like that, my playful girl is back. She trails her hands up my arms, making me growl low as I watch her. "I mean... yes, daddy?"

"That's my good girl." I grip her hips and have her on her back quickly as she giggles. "I need all of you."

"Then take me."

It's all the permission I need. Just like her words in the kitchen about wanting me to take her pretty much anywhere in my damn house, I don't need her to say anymore than that to know she wants me just as much.

I slide her down the bed and settle between her legs. I push her feet up so they're resting on my shoulders as I look down at her. "How do you want it, beautiful?" My voice cracks, but it's because my control is diminishing by the second.

"I want you to show me what it's like to be possessed by a man who cares about me. I want you to wash all of the past memories away so all I know is you and the way you make me feel. That's what I want," she pleads.

I growl possessively and grip my cock. I know just by fingering her that she's tight as hell, and I'll rip her apart if I take her how I want. Instead, I rub the head of my dick through her wetness before sliding into her. Just the tip has her gasping, arching, and rolling her eyes back in her head.

I know instinctively I'm about to be in for a legendary ride.

"More, daddy. Please… Please."

My intention is to thrust in her, bury myself balls deep, and hold myself there until she stretches around my size. I'm thick. Long. Long enough to make my woman have to take a sick day as soon as I'm finished fucking her.

What happens is better than my wildest fantasies. Krissy wraps her legs around my hip, driving me deeper into her than I've ever been in anyone in my life. The groan that comes out of me stems from deep within the pit of my stomach. I keep myself from falling on top of her, but just barely. She feels so fucking good wrapped around me and squeezing my dick, that my entire body is quaking. If I move, I'm coming. I'd rather not embarrass myself before rocking her world.

"Fuck…," I rumble low against her throat. "Fuck, baby, you're so tight. Just give me a second."

"You're not gonna hurt me, daddy. I promise."

I growl against her throat before biting it with a grin. "While not hurting you is my number one concern, not coming right now is right up there." I kiss across her throat to her neck before thrusting slowly. Not exactly how I planned for this to go, but she feels way too good to rush this.

She hums out a moan and wraps her arms around me. She scratches her nails lightly across my back, but she could dig into it. I wouldn't complain at all. I'd probably relish in the pain.

My thrusts might be slow, but I'm making sure to please her in every way I possibly can. I pull all the way out before pushing all the way back in. I up my pace after a few moments. Her pussy is dripping for me and making the most filthy noises, but it turns me on even more. Her moans bring it all home.

Before long, I'm on my knees pounding into her pussy. She meets me thrust for thrust, but I need more. I grab her feet that she's locked around my waist and push them together after lifting them high in the air. Kissing her calves and holding her ankles, I grip her hip and don't stop thrusting.

"Oh... mmmm... Caden...," she moans.

I grin and lift her ass up enough to change the angle of my dick inside her. I slap her ass as I narrow my eyes. I give her a dominant growl and smirk. "If you want to come, you better be a good girl and say my name right."

Her pussy grips my dick tighter when my hand meets her ass. I can see her stomach clench as she moans. "Daddy! Daddy... Daddy... Oh, fuck yes...!"

She clenches and tightens around me uncontrollably as she saturates me and the sheets beneath us. She writhes beneath me like she can't get enough but wants even more.

She can't figure out what to grip, and watching her arch and claw at anything to hold onto just makes me more feral and possessive. "Say you're my girl, baby. Tell me." I thrust into her harder and harder, watching her carefully to make sure it's not too much.

"Yours! All yours!"

"Look at me. Look in my eyes and tell me."

I pull her into each and every thrust, making sure I hit all of her spots that will drive her over the edge while giving her all of me that she can take.

Her eyes snap to mine like such a good girl. "Yours. I'm all yours. All yours!"

"That's my good girl," I rumble appreciatively. "All mine."

To reward her, I release her hip, still holding her legs tight. I grip her tits in turn and pinch her nipples, playing with each of them as I make her forget how to speak. Nothing but unrecognizable mumbles are coming from her throat. Her eyes open and fall closed. I feel her just about to lose control, and it's only then that I let her legs fall open. I keep pounding into her sweet, tight, pretty little pussy and start rubbing her clit with my thumb.

"Daddy!" she screams as she arches off the bed into me, making me sink even deeper. Her pussy walls clench me tight, and my eyes roll back into my head.

"Fuck, baby. Come. Come for daddy. Right now." I add a little more pressure to her clit and rub it faster. "Keep those eyes open for me."

"Daddy!" she shouts again as her walls finally collapse around me and give me what I want. She comes hard for me, the waves of her release washing over her. She rides them and does exactly as I ask. She keeps her eyes open for me, and seeing her come is the sexiest thing I've ever seen in my life.

The moment I feel her reach the peak of her own orgasm, I lean down and take her mouth with mine in a fiery and possessive kiss. As my tongue swipes over hers, I growl deeply as my own release hits. I come harder than I've ever come for anyone and fill her pussy to the brim with everything I have in me to give her.

"Krissy!" I roar as jolt after jolt of electricity shoots down my back and through my dick. Just when I think I'm about to start coming down, she tightens around me and hits a second orgasm, milking everything she can from my cock.

Once I'm sure neither of us are going to explode a third time, I slowly pull myself out of her. I fall on my back next to her and pull her into me. She scrambles until she's as close to me as she possibly can be without actually being inside me. She throws one leg over mine and her arm around my middle. I kiss the top of her head and gently run my fingertips up and down her arm as we both catch our breath.

Several minutes of silence later, Krissy lets out a slow hum of a breath. "I've never been so happy," she whispers against my chest.

I hug her closer and keep soothingly trailing my fingertips up and down her arm and back. "I'll happily make you happy every single day for the rest of my life, sweet girl."

"I'd like that."

"Good. Because that's my life's mission. You're my life's mission."

She hums against my chest and I feel her slowly slip off to sleep. I let her because it's what she needs, but also because I want her at peace. I don't want her thinking of the dark cloud that looms over us.

Chapter Thirteen

♡ Krissy ♡

(Seven Months Later)

"I love you, baby. I won't be long. Just need to finish this up," Caden rumbles.

I smile. I love when he tells me he loves me. "Can't wait to see you. I feel like you've been working so much over the past couple of months."

"I know, baby girl. I'm sorry. But with Ryland missing again, we can't be too careful with you and Jimothy."

I sigh. Ryland. He always manages to show up when things are going so well. "I know. I'm sorry. I just miss you, but I know you're working hard to keep us both safe. I wanted to say a last goodbye to my house anyway."

Caden chuckles. "Make sure Troy's with you."

"I know, my love. It feels weird going anywhere without him now."

"Good. I want it to feel normal for him to be around."

I giggle. "I still wonder if he, Nate, and Jimothy can hear us when we're messing around."

He rumbles low. "You mean if they can hear you screaming 'daddy'?"

I laugh. "Caden!"

"Hey, yeah. I'll be right there. Tell him to wait for me, and I'll head to the call with him."

"You gotta go?"

"Yeah, baby. I'm sorry. We've been trying to bust this asshole who's been shoplifting at the grocery store. Doesn't sound big, but he's at a felony level."

"Wow. For just groceries?"

"Yep. I want to get to the bottom of it. Figure out who it is. Maybe we can help instead of fuck his life up, ya know?"

"I understand. I love how kind you are. I love you, my love. Be safe, okay? See you soon?"

"I'm looking at about an hour. I can finish this paperwork in the morning. I love you, too, baby. See you soon."

We both hang up with those words. We never say goodbye because we don't know what the future holds. We always say that we love each other and we'll see each other soon because, God forbid, anything happens to him or me, we want to make sure that the other knows we love them and will see them soon. No matter what. Even if it's in death, we'll be reunited eventually.

I put my phone in my back pocket and hurry to find Troy. He's waiting by the door. "Ready to go?" I ask. "I figured I can say my goodbyes and then be ready for the Fourth Fest at Walker Ranch by the time Caden gets home."

Troy grins. "First, I'm happy to see you trusting us more and getting out there more. It's nice seeing you open up."

I blush and push some hair behind my ear. "Caden helps with that."

"He might be an asshole, but he's good at making people feel safe."

I laugh. "I love the brotherly love between all of you guys. The camaraderie. It's fun to watch."

"Well, years of practice." Troy grins as he opens the door.

I look back and see Killer snuggled with Jimothy taking a nap. My heart skips a beat, but he looks so content. "Maybe I should leave him be," I mumble.

"You want Killer with us?"

I nibble my lip before shaking my head. "No. Leave him. We won't be long."

"Okay. Let's get there. Want to drive?"

"I kind of want the walk. I've been feeling a little restless."

"Then, we'll walk. You can tell me about how excited you are seeing Lila Rose live and in person." He grins as we start our short trek through the woods.

I laugh. "I'm actually looking forward to it. I keep hearing her new song on the radio when I turn it on. Almost every time. If I don't hear it right away, it'll come on shortly after."

"What do you think of it?"

"It's super good. They always call it the anthem of the Summer. I completely agree. She's super talented. It's still so hard to believe she grew up here. She's got such a star quality that I feel like she should've just been born in Nashville and raised there so she could've grown up in the music industry."

Troy laughs. "Yeah, she went to a lot of record labels. Some, she just sat there singing acapella for them on the sidewalk in front of the building. Got rejected every time. That is until Blake stepped in. Got lucky sitting next to a record exec on the plane to some training he was doing."

"I love that story so much. Blake and Lila are honestly like the American Dream couple. Best friend's little sister turned love of his life."

Troy chuckles. "He was in love with her for fucking years. Never admitted it because he didn't want Keelan to freak out on him and ruin their friendship. You're right there, though. Their love story is right out of a romance novel."

"My favorite kind of romance," I say dreamily.

Troy laughs again. "Don't think you don't have one of your own. Cop supposed to protect the damsel in distress. Ends up falling in love and ruining his brother's virgin ears by making her call him 'daddy'."

I squawk and shove him, thoroughly embarrassed. "Oh my God, tell me you don't hear anything!"

He grins as he laughs, staying steady, even though I pushed him pretty hard. He's like a brick wall. All of the Andrews brothers are. "Ya'll need soundproof fucking walls."

My face heats up. "It's official. You all have to move out."

"I love how you say we have to move out. Already staked claim, I see." He waggles his eyebrows at me, and we both laugh.

"Yep!"

We fall silent for the rest of the walk. He's right. My romance with Caden is a whirlwind, but I'd have it no other way. The past year has been the best of my life. For Valentine's Day, he got me a Symphony bar because he knows they're my favorite, and a bouquet of fire and ice carnations. So simple and probably not what he had originally planned, but I cried. It was the best Valentine's Day gift I've ever received. The day was incredible. Also the best I've ever had. Every day with him is even better than the one before.

Even with Ryland missing. I've barely thought of him. I've started to come out of my shell and feel stronger. While I fear him finding me, I don't fear him as I did.

I sniff the air and furrow my brows, looking at Troy. There are several forest fires burning in Texas. We smell smoke all of the time from every direction, but this seems different. We both stop in our tracks, but it's far too late.

We both see the smoke pouring from my house at the same time we see a black truck parked in the driveway. There's a man standing behind the truck using it to cover him. Troy shoves me down at the same time he's taking out his gun.

"Get down!" he shouts as I hit the ground.

Shots ring out all around me, and I scream as I cover my head. Someone screams. Another person grunts.

Or maybe it's the same person doing both.

I don't dare lift my head. I don't want to see Troy laying on the ground.

I lay frozen in fear, like I really haven't come as far as I have. Ryland.

He's back.

How is he back?

How did he find me? I knew he would, but how?

Suddenly, someone is wrapping my hair around his hand. I know instinctively who it is. I can smell him. A sickening cologne. I've never liked it. Never knew what it was either. I never knew where he even kept it, but I've always hated the smell of it. It smells like a cigar with a hint of vanilla. There's nothing about it that smells mature.

"Get up, bitch. You're fucking mine, now." Ryland's growl is so much darker; more intimidating than Caden's. Caden's sends shivers down my spine in a good way. Ryland's just makes me fear everything that's about to happen to me.

Ryland drags me somewhere that's way too close to the fire. I think he's going to throw me in it, but he doesn't. He shoves me hard against the black truck instead.

"Krissy! Get down!" Troy yells. I try to turn towards him, but Ryland opens the door to the truck and uses my body as a shield. "Drop!"

I try, but Ryland holds me tighter against him, though I'm dead weight in his arms. "I can't!" I scream. I'm starting to panic. If Ryland gets me into the truck, I'm dead. "Let go!" I shriek.

He slaps me hard with the back of his gun. So hard that I see stars. I feel him throw me into the truck, but I can't fight him. He slams the door. I hear more shots and a scream. I don't know if I'm the one screaming, but I stay on the floor of the truck. He can't get to me too easily here. Not if he has to drive.

Unless he shoots me.

It's then I remember my phone. There's still commotion outside, so I quickly grab my phone and dial 911. It's a small town, so they answer fast.

"Nine-One-One, what's your emergency?" a friendly male voice says.

"I'm being kidnapped by Ryland Evans," I say as quickly as possible. "Get Caden Andrews. Please. I'll try to keep my phone on. Please mute yourself. Please, please listen. That's all I can say." I pray they don't ask questions and do what I say. I want them to mute themselves so they can hear everything that's about to happen. I quickly shove the phone in my pocket as more shots ring out. Ryland opens the door and jumps in, howling.

"Fuck! Son of a bitch!"

He stays ducked down as he throws the truck in reverse and peels out of the driveway. I do all I can to stay strong.

Fight.

Survive.

I have way too much to live for to let Ryland win.

Ryland glares at me as he spins out onto the highway. All I can know is that he's speeding North of Piper Falls, and that scares me more than Ryland himself does.

"Ryland, what are you doing?" I almost yell. "There's a forest fire roaring in this direction!"

"Shut the fuck up! Get your ass up here and reach in the back. Find a shirt you can tie around my fucking leg right now! He fucking shot me, you goddamn whore! It's your fault! You're gonna pay for this, cunt!"

I wince at all of the name calling, but I jump into action, hoping against all hope that he doesn't take my phone from me. It's my literal lifeline right now.

I catch a sob in my throat as I find a t-shirt. "Ryland, please. There's a huge fire North of town. They're doing all they can to maintain it, but it's out of control. They've shut down parts of the highways and Interstates. They've evacuated hotels. Homes."

"Shut the hell up and get me the fucking shirt!" he screams. He slaps my leg so hard, I jerk, but I'm grateful he didn't do it higher. He'd have felt my phone.

I grab the shirt and hand it to him as I turn and sit down. He grabs my hair and yanks me towards him. "Are you fucking kidding me? I can't drive and stop the damn bleeding, can I?" He jerks the steering wheel up enough to shove me down into his lap so I can wrap his leg.

His jeans are already saturated with blood. I don't know if Troy hit an artery, but I hope he did. The hole in his pant leg is low. More towards the bottom of his foot. I sniffle because I don't think there's an artery there. But maybe he shattered bone.

I make quick work of dressing his wound. I do it tight because I know if I don't, he'll make me do it again. When I finish, he tugs me away from him and throws me against the passenger side door like I'm nothing. I don't cry. I refuse to. Not only am I stronger than that, but I know it will infuriate him. I have to do everything I can to keep him calm.

I only hope 911 is still on my phone. I sit at an angle, my ass towards the door as I settle as far away from him as I can.

Of course, he sees it almost instantly. "What the fuck are you doing? Sit right, Phoenix. Put your fucking seatbelt on. You want me to get pulled over and end up back in jail?"

Yes, I say to myself.

I choose my spoken words carefully. "I hit my hip on the door when I got in. It hurts really bad, but I want to be able to help you if you need me to. I don't want to sit on it and make it stiff so I can't move."

My answer seems to please him. He gives me a half smile as he keeps driving. If I'd said anything about him hurting me when he threw me in the car, he'd hit me. I need to stay awake. As strong as I can be. Any hit can be life or death for me. I don't know his plans.

I breathe a silent breath of relief, but end up coughing instead. My eyes are starting to burn. The smoke is getting thicker. We're not that far away from the fire right now. I cover my mouth and turn my head from him.

In some kind of bizarre moment of calm, he shows me the side of the man I fell in love with. He takes the water bottle in his cup holder, takes a drink, and gives it to me. "Here. Drink. I have some more at my hideout. We'll be safe from the fire. Just have to get there first."

I keep from biting my tongue. Instead, I force a smile and take it. I wouldn't trust it at all, but I did just watch him take a drink of it. And I'm thirsty. I need something. I know hydration is important. So, I take a drink and just nod.

A few more minutes of silence, and I start to recognize where we're going. I swallow hard. "Um… the hideout…"

"It's not the hotel, if that's what you're thinking. Too easy to track us. Think like a cop. I taught you better, baby."

I swallow the bile that him calling me 'baby' elicits. I take a breath and another drink of the water before putting the lid back on the stainless steel bottle and putting it back down in the cup holder.

"Well, if it's not the hotel, it has to be close to there, right? The fire goes for miles."

He chuckles. "Yes."

I look out the window. The smoke is thick, but I won't drink more water. I think we're going to need it. I say 'we' because I need him to help me survive this. I may not trust him at all, but the one thing I can say is that his survival skills are unlike any other I know. I learned a lot from him about staying alive in situations that aren't normal out in the wilderness. I may have hated it all, but I listened because I knew he wouldn't let himself die. He's too cocky and proud.

"So, you have a hideout outside that can withstand the fire?"

"Near a water source, no less." He grins proudly.

I scan my brain for the lakes and rivers in the area. There aren't many, but near the Crimson Hotel, there's a lake less than a mile away. Crimson Lake. The hotel banks on its guests doing water events during their stay so they can rent equipment and make more money. Caden took me there for New Year's. We celebrated ringing it in with a kiss on a rented yacht in the middle of the lake.

"Near Crimson Lake? So, we can jump in and not die when the fire inevitably reaches us? Because I'm honestly scared of that, Ryland. I trust you. I do. Just not nature. It's unpredictable. You've always said that."

He grins at me proudly. "So, you did listen to shit that I said, huh?" He looks back towards the road.

I don't dare think he can't see me, though, so I hold back the eyeroll and look down and play up the part he loves the most. "I always listened to you, Ryland," I say softly. Submissively. "You were always right. Even if I didn't know it then."

He makes a turn, and I glance up. As I thought, he's turning into the hotel parking lot. There are no cars. I know they've finished evacuations. That means the fire is closer than I thought it was. I thought I had more time. I shouldn't have been so naive.

He turns to me then and puts a hand on my thigh. I keep from jerking away, but barely. "Look, Phoenix." He squeezes my thigh, but I don't look up at him. He likes when I submit. "Baby, I fucked up in the past. I know that. You're the love of my life and greatest loss of it, but we're gonna be okay. I promise. I'm not letting anything hurt you. I'll keep you safe. I have a plan to get us the fuck out of here. Okay? I need you to trust me right now. Can you at least do that for me?"

My heart cries for what he could've been. I've always seen the potential for a good guy there, but I know that's not him. He doesn't have an ounce of good in him. He's a liar. Manipulative. The second we're safe and back in Minnesota, it's over for me. I know he'll kill me.

I'm not going down without a fight. At least Caden will know I died fighting for my life. For the life I want with him.

"Okay," I whisper. "I trust you." *Not a chance. I don't trust you at all. When the fire passes, that's the end of it. One way or another.*

He squeezes my thigh again and gets out of the truck. I follow him, making sure my phone is still where it needs to be. I let out a breath when I feel it. I close the door behind me and keep my ass away from his line of sight so he doesn't see it. I pull my shirt down. It's a skimpy tank top because it's hot, but I've never been more grateful I chose to wear this because it's even hotter here. That means the fire really is close. I can smell the heat from it now. It's almost as overpowering as the smoke itself.

"Let's go." Ryland adjusts his backpack and hands me the water bottle. I notice then that his wound is just a flesh wound. It barely even bothers him. "Don't worry on drinking it if you need to. I have another bottle for us in the backpack and more at my hideout. We're gonna be okay. I promise."

I just nod and follow him after taking the water. I hate that he can sense my fear, but I'm really glad he's here. I wouldn't be able to be out here on my own. Even if I made it to the lake, I wouldn't know what to do. Swim out as far as I can? Risk drowning instead of burning alive? Cover myself with sand? Hide down in the rocks?

I rub my chest and try to focus on following Ryland, but my intrusive thoughts take the lead. Before I know it, all I can see is the fire catching us before we get to the place he believes is safe. I'm not paying attention to anything but if I can see the flames bearing down on us or not. I trip over a root and scream before I can catch myself. I crash to the ground, my ankle caught in the root of the tree.

"Ow!" I yell, immediately grabbing for my ankle. Tears sting my eyes, but it's not from the smoke or the fear. "Oh my God," I groan, a sob escaping as I reach for my foot. I'm sure it's not supposed to be twisted at that angle. My right ankle is twisted towards the left one. I'm flexible, but not enough to make my ankle nearly touch the ground like that. I look up at Ryland, complete fear paralyzing me. "I don't want to die!" I sob, unable to control it over the pain. My foot is shattered. There's no way it isn't.

Ryland glances toward the North as he kneels down. He looks at my foot. "It's broken. You need to let me get you out of here. It's gonna hurt."

"I don't care! Just please don't let me die! Please, Ryland!" I beg. I'm not even acting this time. I'm appealing to his hero side. He loves that, but it doesn't matter to me. I just want to live a little bit longer. Long enough to at least try and escape.

"Okay! Okay, baby. You gotta calm down for me. Okay?"

I nod as I sob uncontrollably and gasp for air. He reaches down for my foot and manages to get it loose, but when he has to twist it just a slight amount, I scream out in pain and cry even harder. I nearly fall backwards as I start seeing black dots in front of me. I do all I can to breathe through it. I can't pass out. I'll die if I do that. I won't have a chance.

I tremble. I want to scream again, but no sound comes out.

He stands and bends to help me up. Once he has me on my feet, I keep my right one up and off the ground. I was right. There's no way it isn't broken. It's bent unnaturally.

"Can you walk?" he smirks. I hate that I know he's joking to try and make me feel better. If he were Caden, I'd swat him. Instead, I just glare. He laughs and turns. He kneels and looks up at me over his shoulder. "I can't carry you like my bride. That'll be later. You need to jump on my back. I have to be able to see the path, and it's getting harder with the thicker smoke. We're almost there." He hands me his backpack.

I put it on and tremble, but do as he says. I don't like that I can't do anything but obey. I put my hands on his shoulders and steady myself while I give him my right leg. He's gonna have to support that one. I can't put weight on it.

He grips me under my thigh as he starts to stand. Like a good girl, I wrap my arms around his shoulders and swing my other leg up. He catches me under my thigh, standing to his full height and adjusting me so he takes most of my weight. I hold onto him tight because I don't have any other choice.

"Please don't let me die," I whisper before I start coughing.

"I won't, Phoenix. I know I'm not good at keeping promises, but I'm keeping that one. I won't let you die."

The smoke is burning my lungs now. I feel myself starting to get closer to blacking out. I do all I can not to, but I don't know how much longer I can fight it.

"I'm not gonna make it, Ryland. I'm gonna pass out."

"No you're not. Breathe into my shirt."

I drop my head and do all I can to breathe in just him. I'll take his disgusting scent over the smoke any day.

He hurries into a cave and moves back into it as deep as he can. It doesn't seem like it's far back enough, but he's confident it is. I have to trust that. I have no other choice.

He kneels down and helps me off him. I can't see anything, but apparently he can. I turn towards the cave entrance and quickly take out my phone as he's distracted.

I push a button on the side.

Nothing.

No light. Nothing.

It's dead, and I don't know when it happened. I don't know if help is coming. I quickly put it back into my pocket just as a flashlight lights the inside of the cave. We're further back from the entrance than I thought, but I still don't know if it's enough.

"It's getting really dark out there, Ryland."

"Don't think about out there. Come here. Let me deal with your foot. Hurry up."

I move as quickly as I can and sit on the rock he's gesturing to. He takes the backpack off me and starts digging in it. He comes out with what looks like an ace bandage and something else that could probably work as a split.

"Oh God," I whisper.

"I don't have anything for the pain." He offers me a piece of fabric. I don't know what it is. "Bite down on this when I say."

I whimper but take it.

He makes quick work of setting up all he needs. I'm wearing shorts and flip flops, so it's not painful to get anything off me because there's nothing in the way.

He grabs my ankle gently and looks at me. "Look at me."

I look at him. I can feel my eyes doing anything but staying still. "Ryland."

"Look at me," he says a little more forcefully. My eyes lock on him. "Don't look at anything else. Just me. Bite down now."

I keep my eyes locked on his and bite down. He rights my ankle, and I see stars. I scream, but my jaw is locked down on the fabric.

"Keep biting down."

I keep screaming into the fabric. My head falls back as I sob. My eyes roll back. The pain is so unbearable, I feel it shooting throughout my entire body straight to my brain. He quickly wraps it and makes sure it's stabilized. I can't stop screaming.

Only now, it's not because of the pain.

It's fear.

The fire is roaring by us. The temperature has raised exponentially. I feel like I might spontaneously combust. Ryland looks over his shoulder and moves quickly over me. His eyes are wide. His mouth is open.

But I see nothing more than that because blackness overtakes me as I fall backwards against the wall of the cave.

Chapter Fourteen

♡ Caden ♡

"Caden!" Annie screams as she runs into my office without knocking on the closed door.

"Holy shit! What! What the fuck?" I jump to my feet and grab her arms before she runs into Mateo, who nearly knocked his chair over as he quickly got up. My heart is racing. This isn't a normal reaction from any of our dispatchers, especially her.

"Caden!" she shouts again. I can tell she's going into shock.

"Annie! What? What happened?" I drop my voice to a more calm tone, deeper, and she looks up at me choking on sobs.

"Krissy! He has Krissy! He has her!"

"What? Who? Who has Krissy?" I know the answer, but I don't want to believe it.

"Ryland Evans! He has her! And a call just came in from Troy saying her house was on fire and he'd been shot!"

My eyes fly to Mateo. He whips out his phone, not needing me to tell him to call my brother while I figure out what the fuck is happening. He follows me out of my office and closes the door behind him as I walk a trembling Annie back towards the dispatch office.

"Who has her call, Annie?"

"Shane!"

"Okay. Okay, honey. You need to be calm for me, okay? Sit right here." I set her down in a chair across from Sebastian, a detective and one of my best friends. He looks at me, confused, but the second he sees my expression and hears Mateo talking to Troy, he immediately stands and moves around his desk to comfort Annie.

Mateo and I walk into the dispatcher room and beeline for Shane. We both grab an extra chair and flip it around so we can both listen to the call as we sit backwards in it.

"She wanted me to mute myself. Listen. I have her heading North. I'm tracking her phone. She said something about Crimson Lake. Broke up a little bit."

"That's right in the path of the fire," Mateo says.

"She's coughing. A lot. I think they're close. He hasn't touched her. He's being nice. She dropped a few clues for us. I took the call. She said his name. Said he was kidnapping her. We heard shots. She told us to mute. We did it because she seemed adamant and terrified. I heard him getting inside screaming at her. We're glad we did because he was a problem at first. We think he got shot and made her dress his wound. Troy was on with another dispatcher. Said he knows he hit Ryland."

"How's my brother?" I look at Mateo as we get up simultaneously.

"Good. FD is there."

"Let's go."

We take off running to my truck. When we get there, we jump in and take off in the direction of Krissy's house that's now burning.

Mateo glances at me. "I think I know you well enough to know you aren't thinking what I think you're not thinking."

"I'm not going into a fire, guns blazing. I'm stopping by the house and getting shit from Blake."

"Thank fuck," Mateo grumbles.

"And dropping you off."

"Like hell you are. I'm going with. Just texted my girl. You're not going in alone. You need someone to have your fucking back. If you get killed up there, I'll never forgive myself, and neither will anyone else."

I take a breath and nod. I want him safe, but I know I'll be better off with him there. We both will. We can watch each other's backs. We always have.

We both fall silent as I speed out of town towards the house. I don't have lights and sirens hooked up to my personal vehicle, so I hope I don't get pulled over. I should ask for an escort, but all I can think of is getting to Blake so I can be as safe as possible while going after Krissy.

I take the turn into Krissy's driveway and slam on my brakes behind the fire rig. Mateo and I jump out, and run towards Blake. The house is fully engulfed, but I don't care.

"Blake!" I bark.

He turns, sees me, and yells to Keelan. "Mancini! Take command!"

"On it!"

Blake jogs towards me. "Before you say anything, I know." He opens the back of the truck and throws two bags of stuff at me and Mateo before taking out a third one.

"What are you doing?"

"You think for a fucking second you're going up there without me? In the bag is a fire shelter. I made the department get them for us last year just in case we had to go out and fight a forest fire. Coming in handy right now, huh?"

I notice his bag is smaller. "Why are mine and Mateo's bigger?"

"Pants." He pats his. "I don't have extra coats, but it doesn't matter. We have the shelters if things get dicey." He takes his helmet and jacket off. He hangs it on the back of the rig.

Mateo and I open the bag and quickly pull out the pants. We quickly put them on. "Oxygen?" Mateo asks.

Blake shakes his head. "No. If we need to deploy the fire shelters, oxygen isn't going to do shit but make it worse for us. We'll need to dig a hole in the dirt to breathe." He nods to the truck. "Let's move. You're about to get a crash course in using these. If we need to use them, it's because shit is about to get real fucking bad."

Let's hope that doesn't happen," I mumble, jumping into my truck. Blake gets in the passenger side. Mateo leaps into the back. I look over my shoulder and peel out onto the highway.

Blake texts someone. I'm sure it's Lila. He knows the danger we're about to go into and wants to make sure she knows he loves her. Mateo is doing the same thing, and I wish upon every unseen star that we make it in time. I hate that these two are being put into danger, but I've never been more grateful to have such a good team.

Just as I get to the road, I see a Piper Falls squad car whip to the side. It's Melony Daniels, the Sergeant working today. She waves and keys the mic of her radio. "State Patrol is right behind me. He's gonna escort you. I'm following. We think her phone died, but we know she's at the Crimson Hotel."

Blake grabs my radio. "Tell me you're kidding! The Crimson Hotel was evacuated hours ago! The fire was less than five miles away when I checked on it over two hours ago!"

"No, sir," Melony says. "Not joking. She said that's where they were. Her phone died just after they started hiking somewhere. We heard Ryland say he's got a hideout."

"A hideout? What the fuck is some bullshit hideout gonna do if they're in the goddamn middle of a forest fire!" Mateo roars. It's exactly what I'm thinking, but I don't respond. State Patrol is speeding towards us, and I'm ready to follow.

As he barrels by, I fly out after him. Melony follows. Both of them have lights and sirens blaring. I grab my radio from Blake. "When we get there, get out," I command. "I don't want you guys there in harm's way. We have Blake. That's enough bodies to worry about."

"Not a chance, Lieutenant," Melony says.

"That's a direct order, Sergeant. Disobey, I'll put a letter in your jacket and have you suspended." It's not something I want to say, but I don't want her near this. "You have a family, Melony."

"With all due respect, Caden, so do you."

I sigh. "Please. Please just obey me on this one." I've never pleaded for anything in my life, but I will on this.

"We'll back off, Lieutenant," the State Patrol cop says. I recognize the voice, but can't place his name. "But don't you think for a second you'll be in there alone. I'm already notifying rescue and water planes to be on the lookout for you."

"Thank you," I say, my voice cracking.

"You got it, sir. Just bring that girl back alive. And bring yourselves back alive, too, ya hear?"

"Loud and clear. Don't let Melony disobey. She'll try."

"I'll take care of it, sir. I promise you that."

It takes very little time to get there. When we do, we park my truck next to a black one. Melony, like I thought, tries to get out of her squad, and succeeds, only to have her ass hauled into the State Patrol's squad.

"No! Caden! Goddammit! Don't do this! It's way too close!" she yells to me.

"In the car, Daniels!" I bark as I jump out. She yells more as State closes the door on her. She's in the back, so she can't get out even if she wanted to. Not from the inside anyway.

"We don't have time, Caden," Blake says. "He's got her. We need to move. It's fucking hot. The fire is close. Way too close."

"Then we run," Mateo says.

"No," Blake responds. "We walk quickly and safely. Running could kill us. Especially if someone falls. The smoke is thick. We need to be vigilant. Flashlights out of the pack. Let's go."

We all grab the lights out of the pack as we walk, then throw the pack over our shoulders like a backpack. We walk quickly, but keep our eyes peeled. He's right. The heat is getting intense. Blake showed us how to use the shelters while we were driving. We only saw once and never got to try, so we don't have the muscle memory Blake has, but I hope to hell instincts kick in if we need it.

The smoke gets thicker. It's not long we've been walking, but already our eyes are stinging and watering. We're all coughing.

"No oxygen was a bad idea," I say before coughing again.

"Oxygen can explode under hot temps," Blake says. "Like what we're about to face. Take out the water from your packs and the white cloth. Keep moving."

We obey and watch him for every single action we're supposed to take. He takes a long drink of the water before saturating the cloth and tying it around his mouth and nose like a bandana. Mateo and I do the same thing. He keeps the bottle and puts it in his pocket as he walks.

"We don't want any extra fuel for the fire around us. See the ground? It's orange. That means we've already had a plane fly through here with the retardant. This area won't burn, but the surrounding areas will. We need to stay in the area with the retardant. There's a cave up here. When you said hideout, this was my thought."

I let out a breath. "Fuck. A cave? So, she'll be good, then."

"Not necessarily. Caves are all different. You never know how they're structured. If it's rock, she'll probably survive unless there's methane gasses or something." He coughs. "Common in caves, but not in that one. I used to go up there all the time with my brother when we were kids and our parents took us here. The cave has rock walls and a dirt floor. There's vines around it that will burn. If they catch, some go inside the cave entrance, which means the flames will, too." He coughs more. His throat is raspy. "Even if it doesn't, the fire will go by and eat all the oxygen. The cave isn't safe unless she gets down on the ground and digs a hole to breathe in. And she needs to be far back to avoid as much heat as possible. It's the heat that will do the most damage." More coughing.

"Great," I growl, vowing to kill Ryland myself as I cough hard.

"It's getting louder!" Mateo shouts over the increasing roar a few moments later before he starts coughing.

I look to Blake. "What do we do, man?"

He looks around. "The cave is really close, but we're not gonna make it. The heat is increasing. We've only got a minute or so. Maybe less." He drops to his knees and starts digging a hole. "Caden, there! Mateo, there!" He points to either side of him. More coughing out of all of us.

Still, we both drop and mimic his every move. Each time he looks around, we do the same, but none of us stop digging until he says.

"I'm starting to see flames, man!" Mateo yells.

"Shelters!" Blake commands.

I pray like hell we're doing it right. Just like he said, we pull it out and cover ourselves with it like a blanket. We tuck it under our bodies, holding the corners with our hands and feet as well as the rest of us. I can feel the wind pick up, but I know that's not what it is. It's the flames. They feel like they're going right over the top of us. It sounds like a flight of fucking fighter jets all flying low to the ground at the same time.

I close my eyes and think of Krissy as I shove my face into the hole I dug. I breathe as calmly as I can and focus on how beautiful she is. How sweet and kind she is. How I want to spend the rest of my life with her. I refuse to let this be the end. It won't be. Not until I get to tell her I love her while holding her close.

The wind dies down. The sound dissipates.

And I hear an earth-shattering scream pierce through my heart.

"Krissy!" I shout, unable to choke the words down.

"Let's move!" Blake shouts. "Leave the shelters! They're done! Can't be reused! Too much noise for this to be over!"

I quickly jump up. We all leave the shelter and quickly move towards the sound. We hear another scream.

"Oh my God," I choke out.

"Don't!" Mateo barks. He drops a hand on my shoulder. "We're close, but we don't know what we're walking into."

I nod and force Blake behind us. I can see the cave. I take the lead, removing my gun from my hip holster. Blake made sure to assure us we'd be okay with it as long as we kept it on our hip so we could lay flat on the ground.

Mateo follows me. He peeks around my shoulder and nods, telling me it's okay for me to make my entrance.

"Don't move!" Ryland is on top of Krissy, and my heart shatters. "Get off her, you motherfucker!"

"Caden!" Krissy shrieks.

"Get off her!" I bark.

"Caden! Get him off! He's dead! He's dead!" She screams again, but it's in panic as she tries to push his heavy body off her.

"We need to go! Now!" Blake shouts.

Mateo and I run towards Ryland and Krissy. We both shove Ryland off. I grab Krissy as Mateo checks for a pulse. "He's still breathing, Blake!" Mateo shouts.

Blake keeps an eye on the sky. "Pull him out! Hurry up!"

Krissy shrieks and nearly falls when I have her on her feet. She cries, and I hate everything about what's happening. "Baby, we need to run. Understand?"

"Just leave me, then! Get out!"

"What?" I grip her wrists when she shoves me. She almost falls back, but I keep her upright, steadying her. "What the fuck are you talking about? Let's go!"

"It's broken, Caden!" she sobs. "I can't run! Just go! Get out of here!"

"I'm not fucking leaving you!" I yell dominantly. She needs that to calm down, and like a charm, it works. "You need to hold on, Krissy," I say, my voice far lower and calmer so she knows I'm not only not angry with her, but also not going anywhere without her. "We need to run. You got it?" I turn and kneel so she can climb on my back. "Get on, baby. Hurry up. I'm not leaving without you."

I hand her my pack. She puts it on fast and hurries to do what I say, but she's still sobbing her heart out, and it crushes my soul. She wraps around me as much as she can, but I got her. Even if she can't hold on with her legs at all, I'm not letting her go.

I run to the edge of the cave where Mateo has just reached Blake with Ryland. Blake leans down and checks Ryland's pulse. "Nope. It's not strong enough, and we need to get to the lake. We can't survive with him as dead weight. He'll either drown us, or we won't be able to get out far enough before the flames hit. He's got burns on his back and arms. He'll be dead before the flames hit anyway."

For the first time in both mine and Mateo's lives, we leave a man behind and run after Blake towards the lake. It's only about a hundred yards, but it looks like miles. Ryland might be a bad guy, but I'd still never leave a man down. The only reason I am is because I'm trusting Blake to make the decision. If he says he's not making it, then I believe him.

"Don't look behind us, baby," I say to Krissy. I can hear the flames bearing down on us; feel the heat from them. Krissy buries her face in my neck and shoulder.

Mateo keeps pace with me as Blake pushes us both forward as quickly as we all can move. The cloth around our faces is long gone. We all took them off after we started running towards the cave. They were bone dry anyway.

"Krissy, listen to me," Blake says. "When we get to that water, we need to strip what we can as quickly as we can. Extra clothes will weigh us down." He coughs, just as we all are. "Then, we need to swim out as far as we can. I need you to hold onto me and Caden, okay? You need to hold onto our waistband. Mateo is the strongest swimmer. We need him to spot us both in case we struggle."

After Krissy finishes her coughing fit, I feel her nod. We reach the water, and I set her down. She doesn't put her right foot on the ground, and I see it's wrapped up pretty good. Maybe I'll have to thank the fucker for that when I see him in hell.

I unbutton her shorts as she tears off her tank top. I help her out of her flip flop, I don't know where the second one is, then quickly start removing my clothes. We all strip down to our underwear, keeping an eye out for the inferno chasing us. We're all coughing and out of breath. My lungs are burning, so I know everyone else's is, as well.

"Getting too close!" Mateo shouts when the roaring gets loud again. "Let's go! In the water!"

"Couldn't have said it better!" Blake shouts back.

I put my gunbelt on. Mateo gives Blake his so he can put it on. We'd rather keep it on us than risk the fire hitting it and setting it off so it randomly starts shooting off an entire clip of bullets at us. The gun will be ruined by the water, but it's still the best option.

I lift Krissy and wade into the water with her. I hiss because it's fucking cold, but it doesn't matter. It feels good against the heat, and it's our only option to survive the mess Ryland put us in.

"You're gonna grab onto our gunbelts, baby. Understand?" I kiss her lips to both comfort her and myself. That's why Blake is wearing Mateo's. It's easier to grab onto that than underwear.

She nods into me. When we get out far enough for the water to hit our waists, I set Krissy down. I help her kneel down, making sure she has our belts. We both start swimming, swiftly cutting through the water. We pull Krissy, who keeps her head above water, but barely.

"Kick one foot, Krissy!" Mateo calls. "It'll balance you!"

I feel the moment she does it because she feels lighter, and I don't hear her sputtering water. The momentum she gets allows us to swim faster, getting further and further away from the shore, but it doesn't feel far enough.

I look over my shoulder quickly, and see the flames are just hitting the treeline at the shore. They're shooting high in the air but have avoided the part where the fire retardant is. It's amazing to look at but scary as hell.

"Far enough?" I ask Blake. Krissy is getting tired. I feel her starting to drag.

"No!" Blake calls. "The water will heat up close to shore. We need to be further out. More in the middle."

I follow his directions. When I feel him slow, I do the same. Krissy is panting. Mateo swims the rest of the way towards us as we turn towards the flames. The air feels heavier. I pull Krissy towards me, so I can keep her close, but also help support her.

After several moments of us catching our breath and lost in our own thoughts as we tread water, I hear what sounds like an engine. We all look up and see a water plane.

"Holy fuck, they did it," Blake says on a relieved sigh as he starts waving. He's talking about the State Patrol and my Sergeant. I couldn't be more fucking proud or grateful. Mateo and I both join in waving. Krissy tries, but she's using all of her energy to stay afloat. She's still coughing, and it sounds bad. Even Blake is watching her closely.

The pilot tips the wing of the plane at us, and I'm hoping that means he saw us. He flies around us and dips low to pick up water. There's no possible way he doesn't see us now, and as he flies back up, he tips his wing again.

"I hope that means we're about to be saved," Krissy says, shivering before coughing more.

"That's exactly what that means." I don't believe in lying, but even if I weren't sure of it, I'd tell her that right now just so she'd be at ease.

"Good," she rasps out before coughing more.

I'd have her drink the water from the lake, but I'm not sure just how safe it is.

I look up when I hear the blades of a chopper. "Jesus Christ," I say. "Fuck, thank you."

The helicopter hovers low, and two swimmers drop down. They swim towards us. "Hey, I'm Luke," one of them says. "This is Jake. We got word ya'll might need some help."

"Fuck, are we glad to see, ya'll," Mateo says. "Get Krissy up first. Broken ankle."

"You got it." Jake signals for the basket. It drops down with the assistance of someone in the chopper.

"I don't wanna go without you," Krissy says, looking up at me.

I lean down and give her a soothing kiss. "I'm right behind you, baby. I promise."

She searches my eyes before reluctantly letting go of me. She lets Jake and Luke help her into the basket. Once they have her steady, Luke looks up and nods. "Two. We need one more of ya'll in here."

"Caden," Blake says. "She needs him."

I don't argue. I just do what I'm told and get in the basket. I wrap my arms around her as they command me to do and relax on the way up. A few moments later, after we're unloaded and a medic is tending to my girl and giving me oxygen, Mateo and Blake make their way up, followed by Luke and Jake. All four of us are tended to and given water and oxygen as they fly us all to the hospital.

I hug Krissy close to me, vowing to never again let her go.

Epilogue

♡ Krissy ♡

(One Month Later)

"Mmm…," I moan as I yawn. Caden's arms tighten around me, and I giggle. "I do actually need to use the bathroom. And a shower sounds amazing."

"I told you when they were fixing your broken ankle that I wasn't letting you go ever again, baby girl."

"Then…, I guess you'll just have to help me."

He smiles into my neck. "Help you shower? See you naked? Make you scream my name while I lick that pretty pussy? Yes, please."

I laugh. "Caden! Behave."

"Word not in vocabulary," he says in a mono robot voice. "Word not in database. Malfunction. Malfunction."

I giggle as he peppers my neck in kisses. "So bad."

"That's better," he growls against my shoulder. I giggle again as he gets up. "Alright, beautiful. If a shower is what you want, I'm happy to help." He slips his arms under my body and scoops me into his arms. He kisses me as I cuddle into him.

"Mmm… Perfect."

This past month has been incredible. The weight of knowing Ryland isn't chasing me has lifted. I feel a thousand times more like myself again.

Jimothy even seems different. We still have no idea how Ryland even knew about him, but we know that he became a target the second Ryland found him. He was chasing down leads for a while, but it seems like he always somehow managed to find his way to Piper Falls in some way. One of Troy's people found out that the reason he went to Dallas is because he figured out about my house. He went to the Dallas branch of the firm my grandparents work with. He wooed a secretary to get him information he needed.

When he found what he needed, he started making a plan. He'd come down here a few times sniffing things out, but he always somehow managed to slip through Troy's guys. It's like he knew they were following. No matter how much they tried not to underestimate him, they did. He was a lot smarter than they thought, even more than I thought.

As soon as I finish going to the bathroom, Caden helps me out of my clothes and into the bath chair he bought for me to use. He covers my casted foot in plastic before grabbing the showerhead and turning on the water.

"How happy are you to get that thing off?"

I groan. "Next month can't possibly come fast enough. I hate everything about this. I want a real bath and shower. One where I can actually, you know, not make you have to help."

Caden laughs. "Baby, if you think this is a problem for me, I don't think you know me very well." He leans down and kisses me.

I giggle and let him do his thing. I learned quickly to let him help. Not only does it help me, but it makes him happy. I love seeing him smile.

We've both been smiling more and more. Jimothy is excited that he got accepted to the University of Texas in Austin. It wasn't originally his first choice, but after he got away from the assholes who adopted him, he decided he wanted to stay close to his real family. Me and Caden.

He's even gotten to meet his grandparents, who flew down here just a few days after our ordeal ended.

Annie, who has become a really good friend, visited me the day I was released from the hospital. She brought homemade soup for us. It was the best chicken noodle soup I'd ever had. She's the sweetest person, and I'm so happy we got to meet.

I even got to meet Shane. I credit him and Annie for assisting in saving my life. He remained very calm and gained all the information needed to help me. Annie knew to get Caden.

But it's mostly Caden, Mateo, and Blake that I've become the closest with. No one but them can understand the ordeal I faced up there because they faced it, too. When the first wave of fire hit, I couldn't believe what I was seeing. The flames reached inside the cave, but didn't get to me.

That was because of Ryland. I still don't understand exactly why he did what he did, but he kept his promise. He shielded me from the flames. I was able to breathe him in instead of the heat. It felt like my lungs were burning, but thanks to him, they didn't, though, I did have a lot of smoke inhalation. He didn't let me die. I'm sure he wanted me to die at his hands, not at the hands of nature, but his last act was saving my life.

Blake told me Ryland's shirt was burned into his skin. His pulse was so weak, he wouldn't have lived much longer. It helped to ease the guilt I had of leaving him there. Despite what he did to me, I'd have rather he been arrested and punished for his crimes. No lenient sentence. Just have the book thrown at him. I felt better knowing that he was more than likely dead before the flames got back.

The first time they hit him, I didn't even know. He didn't scream. He just covered me. His body was recovered, and his autopsy showed a heart attack. I hope that happened before he was burned at all. I may hate him, but I'd never wish that kind of death on anyone.

Troy and Nate moved out of the house. Jimothy is moving into dorms, but I plan on using the insurance money from the house that my grandparents gave me to rebuild my house. He wants to be close, and Caden and I want him close, too.

As for me and Caden, things with us are better than even in my wildest fantasies. He takes care of my every need in the bedroom and out. He never lets me get too deep in my head, but my favorite thing is how he encourages me to do everything I want to do. He never gets pissed at me if I don't make my goal. He just stands beside me while I try again. He's both my biggest cheerleader and my best friend. The fact that I get to call him mine is a bonus.

He kisses my shoulder when he finishes my hair. "Marry me," he rumbles against my throat before he kisses it.

"Wh-what?" I suck in a breath. I don't dare think I heard those words correctly.

He grins against my skin. "I love the way you look when you're lost in thought. I love everything about you, right down to how you call me 'daddy' when you need be fucked and not made love to." He pulls back and shuts the water off. He wraps a towel around me and kisses me as he takes my hands in his. "I love the cute way you snore. I love how excited you get when Killer snuggles with you. I love how happy you look when I walk in the door. How excited you get to tell me about your day. I love the way you listen to me talk about my day. Even though it has to suck to hear about that hard shit, you still never let me hold things back from you." He kisses my nose and squeezes my hands. "I love you. I can't see my future without you in it. Please marry me."

I nod before a huge grin plasters my face. "Yes!" I shout happily while throwing my arms around him. "Yes, Caden. I'll marry you! I'll marry you right now if that's what you want."

He hugs me tight and kisses me deeply, passionately, stealing my breath with his intensity as he possesses all of my soul.

When he pulls away, it's slow. "I can't wait to marry you, but we're doing it right. I want you to have the wedding of your dreams. I'd give you the world if you asked for it, baby." He hugs me again before helping me to stand so he can dry me off. He helps me brush my hair before laying me down and making the sweetest love to me that I've ever felt.

By the time the waves crash over us both, our hearts seem to have completely tied themselves to each other's.

Caden reaches over and slips a ring on my hand as he snuggles me into him. It's a platinum band with a single diamond in the center of six other smaller diamonds, three on each side of the larger one. I recognize it as a Thin Blue Line ring.

Caden kisses me then the ring before hugging me tight. "I know it might not be exactly what you wanted, considering what it reminds you of, but I think it represents a full circle. The Thin Blue Line was once your enemy. Now you're a part of it. Protected by it. The real one. Not the corrupt one. The Thin Blue Line is not cops protecting all bad cops from bad shit. It's cops protecting good cops from bad shit while also protecting their families. Taking care of one another, especially in trying times."

His explanation makes me tear up. "I love it so much, Caden. I love you so much. I wouldn't be here without you and the line this ring represents. It's perfect."

He smiles and cups my cheek. He leans down and kisses me. I sink into him, all thoughts in my mind quieted and only of him and our future.

As he holds me, I know that the rest of our lives will be filled with all of the love and passion either of us could have ever asked for and far more than what either of us could imagine. I can't wait for our future.

And it starts today.

The End

Piper Falls: Station 28 Series

Available Now

Embracing My Duty by Melony Ann
Torn By My Duty by Kayla Baker
Against My Duty by Anneke Boshoff
Defying My Duty by D.L. Howe
Leave Of My Duty by Nikki A. Lamers
Fulfilling My Duty by Havana Wilder
Following My Duty by Louise Murchie
Replete In My Duty by Stacy Kristen
Accepting My Duty by Darley Collins

Other Books By Melony Ann
The Beautiful Dream Series

Available Now

Loving You
My Love, My Heart
Softening Lyric
Undercover Temptations
Captain Charming
Breaking Boundaries
Crashing Into You
Tactical Inferno
Ravishing Our Queen
Cherished By The Texan
Unveiling Our Passions

Box Sets Available

The Beautiful Dream Series: Box Set: Part 1
The Beautiful Dream Series: Box Set: Part 2

The Crane Family Series

Available Now

The Reluctant Mafia King
Sweet Lies
Billion Dollar Love Story
Be Mine
Protecting Her
Dangerously Forbidden Love
His Heart
Love In The Dark

Box Sets Available

The Crane Family Series

The Deimos Trilogy

Available Now

Connor's Legacy
Aryan's Alpha
Kade's Redemption

Box Sets Available

The Deimos Trilogy

The Forbidden Temptation Series

Available Now

The Detective's Forbidden Temptation
The Running Back's Forbidden Temptation

The Lucinio Family Series

Available Now

Rising From The Ashes
The Player's Rebel
Encrypting My Heart
Fighting My Fate
Phoenix Rising
Defending Her Honor

Multi Author Series
Piper Falls: Firehouse 49

Available Now

Ignite My Fire by Melony Ann
Regain My Fire by Kindra White
Playing With My Fire by D.L. Howe
Fight My Fire by Darley Collins
Against My Fire by Anneke Boshoff
Relight My Fire by Louise Murchie
Harness My Fire by Ayana Lisbet
Quench My Fire by Havana Wilder

Let's Be Friends

Follow me on

Bookbub

Facebook

Goodreads

Instagram

Tik Tok

Visit my website
www.melonyannauthor.com

Subscribe to my newsletter and get a FREE never-seen-before NOVELLA just for subscribers!
https://www.melonyannauthor.com/exclusive-content

Join my Facebook Reader Group!
Melony Ann's Sizzling Book Nook

The official Embracing My Duty playlist on You Tube!
https://www.youtube.com/playlist?list=PLpIrYB68evfLE865A0EPZ8QE_W9UDrnE3

Dedication

To all the sexy daddy's out there.

Acknowledgements

To my loves.

To my friends.

To my team.

To the Bookstagram Community.

To my family.

To all of those who believe in me and support me.

To all of those who don't.

Cover by: Carter Cover Designs

Edited by: Alyssa Skaggs

About Melony Ann

Melony Ann began writing short stories and poetry as a child. She continued honing her craft over the years until she took the plunge and began publishing her work, despite having severe anxiety.

Melony is an award winning author, winning a coveted Firebird Award, and writes contemporary romance stories that are full of suspense and a lot of steam.

When she isn't writing, she is loving her family and working to make her life something she deserves.

Melony believes that if her writing can inspire just one person, then all of her hard work is worth it.

Her hope is that her writing allows each and every one of her readers to escape for a little while. To dive into a different world one book at a time.